BATHSHEBA

Also by James R. Shott
in Large Print:

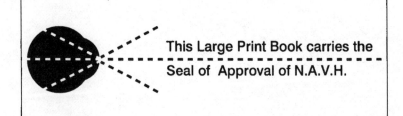

Bathsheba

James R. Shott

Thorndike Press • Waterville, Maine

Copyright © 1996 by Herald Press, Scottdale, Pa. 15683
People of the Promise Book 8

Published in 2003 by arrangement with Herald Press, a
division of Mennonite Publishing House, Inc.

Thorndike Press® Large Print Christian Fiction Series.

The tree indicium is a trademark of Thorndike Press.

The text of this Large Print edition is unabridged.
Other aspects of the book may vary from the original edition.

Set in 16 pt. Plantin.

Printed in the United States on permanent paper.

Library of Congress Cataloging-in-Publication Data

Shott, James R., 1925–
    Bathsheba / James R. Shott.
      p. cm.
    ISBN 0-7862-4534-4 (lg. print : hc : alk. paper)
    1. Bathsheba (Biblical figure) — Fiction. 2. Bible. O.T.
— History of Biblical events — Fiction. 3. Women in the
Bible — Fiction. 4. Large type books. I. Title.
PS3569.H598 B38 2003
    813'.54—dc21   2002190708

To my Critique Group:
Chuck, Barbara, Carolyn,
Stephanie, Ken, and Diana.
They have helped me become a
writer in more ways than they realize.

1

"Queen Abigail is dead!"

Holding his helmet in his hand, Uriah the Hittite stood at the gate of his house, facing the broad courtyard. His usually black curly hair and beard now appeared white because of the ashes he had thrown over himself. His clothes underneath his armor were in tatters. Tears had traced muddy pathways down his face.

His wife, Bathsheba, stood on the rooftop looking down into the courtyard. She nodded. Uriah's announcement was not unexpected. Queen Abigail had struggled with the fever for a month, and in the latest rumors everyone had given up hope for her recovery.

Bathsheba tore her dress. She had heard the keening and wailing from the palace next door and guessed what had happened. Just a moment ago she had changed into an old dress. No use ruining one of her good ones.

She lifted her voice in a mournful cry.

"Oh, my queen! The light of Israel! Beloved of David! First wife of the royal household! Oh! Oh! Oh!"

She had placed on the parapet a bowl of ashes as she waited for her husband to come home to make his announcement. Now she snatched up a handful and threw it on her head, then covered her dress with another handful. How she hated this; it made her feel gritty and soiled. Tonight, after the customary period of mourning, she would have her servant Hephzibah prepare a bath on the rooftop. She would wait until after dark, however. Since the completion of the palace next door, the rooftop no longer afforded her privacy during daylight hours.

But for now, she must appear devastated. She intoned a low moan, careful not to strain her voice — or she would not be able to talk tomorrow.

"Come, wife!" Uriah's voice cracked with genuine sorrow. "We must go immediately to the palace. The king needs us."

Bathsheba descended the steps to the courtyard, wailing but not straining. Her husband's grief was obviously genuine. Not for Abigail, whom he scarcely knew, but for David, whom he loved. In fact, Bathsheba thought bitterly, he loved

David more than her.

Uriah the Hittite, she discovered long ago, had three loves: war, the king and herself. In that order. His huge sword was always by his side, and he wore his helmet, breastplate, and greaves day and night — except to bed, fortunately, since she shared the bed with him.

As she approached her husband across the courtyard, she noted the red-rimmed eyes, the agonized facial expression, the voice already hoarse from expressing sorrow. Would he mourn that intensely for her if she died? Probably not. He would not miss her, as long as he followed his ambitious king into battle.

Bathsheba trailed meekly behind as Uriah led the way to the palace next door. The new palace. Built lovingly by the king for his favorite wife, Abigail. When the fever struck her last month in Hebron, she demanded to be moved to Jerusalem. She seemed to know the fever would murder her, and she wanted to die in her new home.

The palace was magnificent. As soon as the Tyrian builders began laying its foundation, Bathsheba had pressured her husband to claim the Jebusite house next door. He had done so willingly, to be near his king.

She had moved in immediately, knowing she would be very much a part of the society of the royal household. Standing on the front corner of her rooftop, she could see everyone who entered and exited the palace gates. And because her husband was a high-ranking officer, one of the king's Mighty Thirty, she would often be invited to court functions.

Now she climbed the polished limestone steps. Before her loomed the iron gates between two stone pillars.

She always enjoyed this moment, entering the new royal palace. She had done it several times before when it was in the building stages, and once after its completion when Uriah had given her a personal tour. She had fantasized each time that it was her palace, that she — not Abigail — was queen of Israel. She did so now.

She breathed deeply, inhaling the sweet smell of cedar. Everything was new-building clean — the polished limestone floors, the cedar paneling in the vast Assembly Hall, the tapestries on the walls. Sunlight filtered through openings near the ceiling. Colors flirted with each other: the reddish gold of the cedar, the reds and blues of the tapestries, the sparkling white of the floor.

Her home. *Her* palace. *She* was queen of Israel. She was the beloved of David, Anointed One of Yahweh. Ah . . . if only it were true.

The Assembly Hall was filled with people who had come to pay their respects to the king. Each person looked disheveled, which was proper. The men were bareheaded, their hair and beards unoiled and gray with ashes, their clothing dirty and torn. The women, who hovered around the edges to give the men the more prominent places, were dirty and ragged. Grief echoed around the room in high-pitched keening and low-voiced groaning, in wails, moans, sobs, sniffles.

Sorrow doesn't bring out the best in a person's appearance, mused Bathsheba as she forced tears from her eyes and soft cries from her throat.

Her eyes went to the throne on the dais against the back wall, huge, majestic . . . and lonely. She had never seen the king on that throne. He belonged there. He was the chosen of Yahweh, lifted by a providential hand to lead the people of Israel to their destiny. No one else in Israel could comfortably sit on that throne. But it was empty now.

On the dais near the throne stood

Ahitophel, her grandfather, one of David's most respected counselors. She had never felt much affection for him, nor he for her. He was always too busy, and he seemed to disapprove of her marriage to a foreigner.

Bathsheba looked around at the throng of people who had come to the palace to pay their respects to the bereaved king. Everybody who mattered was there. The Mighty Three. The Mighty Thirty. David's closest friends and advisers were military men. There was Joab, his commander-in-chief. And Benaiah, captain of his body-guard. Abishai, Joab's brother. And Shammah. And Hezro. And Eleazar. And Adino. And her husband, Uriah the Hittite. All legends. Rugged, muscular men, bronzed by outdoor living, skilled in their craft — which was warfare. Now emasculated by grief.

And there was Nathan the Prophet. Bathsheba shrank into the background as he marched through the Assembly Hall. People gave way before him.

He — and he only — was not distorted by grief. He looked the same as usual: hair uncombed, beard unoiled, dirty face, his clothes in rags.

He was Yahweh's prophet.

Bathsheba had seen him before. About

two weeks ago, he had stalked past her on a street in Jerusalem. His wild fanatic eyes had stared at her disapprovingly. No wonder nobody liked him, although everybody feared him. He was so negative, always denouncing sin, never supportive.

There he was now, striding through the Assembly Hall as people shrank from him. "Where's Yahweh's Anointed?" he demanded.

Joab, the bold soldier, was the only one who dared to answer. He faced the intimidating man of God and growled, "He's grieving. Let him alone."

Nathan's beard jutted forward; his eyes narrowed. He snapped, "The tomb is ready. Time to go."

Joab stood his ground. "He knows that. He'll come when he's ready."

Nathan hesitated. He probably would have barged off through the halls looking for David, but his dignity might have suffered. Bathsheba smiled. Even fanatical prophets are aware of their dignity.

But someone should tell David that his people were waiting for him to come out and lead the funeral procession to the tomb. Nobody seemed inclined to go. Instead, they just stood in groups, moaning and wailing . . . and useless.

I'll go, decided Bathsheba. *I know where he is.*

Not long ago Uriah had given her a tour of the palace, just after its completion but before anybody had moved in. She had explored every corner of the empty palace, marking in her mind every room. She knew them by heart. She remembered the big room on the third floor, the one with the massive bed, luxuriously appointed, which they called the Queen's Room. And that was where David would be right now.

Quietly she detached herself from the mourners in the Assembly Hall and slipped out of the room. The hall led directly to a stairway, and she climbed to the third floor. Nobody was in the halls; in fact she saw no one anywhere. She went directly to the Queen's Room.

David was there. Alone except for the corpse on the bed.

He sat by the window overlooking the courtyard in the center of the palace. He sat motionless, staring out the window. No tears. No moaning. He just . . . sat there.

Bathsheba glanced at the form on the bed. Her white face, once pretty, now seemed shrunken and old. Flecks of silver touched her temples. The fever had aged her, suddenly. When Bathsheba had last seen her, in Hebron, she had been young, vibrant, and beautiful.

Now she was dead. The only wife, according to common gossip, whom David loved.

Bathsheba chose her words carefully, not wishing to startle him. "It is time, my lord," she said softly.

He nodded but did not turn to look at her. Perhaps he assumed it was one of his wives. He didn't move.

"They are waiting," she added.

"Let them wait."

The words were spoken with such bitterness and anger that Bathsheba gasped. The depth of his grief was more than anyone had realized.

She looked at him then, the quiet figure huddled in front of the window. His linen robe was in tatters. His fair hair and beard, usually oiled and combed, were disheveled and dirty. His shoulders slumped.

Bathsheba's heart went out to him. She longed to rush forward, take him in her arms, kiss away his tears, offer comfort however he wished. But she couldn't. She must not. She could only stand in the doorway and speak softly.

"You are Yahweh's Anointed," she said. "Your people need you. You must go."

15

"No." His word was strained, barely audible. "Not without *her* by my side."

"You must learn to walk alone, my king. Without her. She cannot walk with you."

"Then I must go to her."

"You can't. You are Yahweh's Anointed. You must not forget that."

He sat silent and unmoving for another long moment. Finally he sighed.

"Yes, I know. It is my burden."

"We will help you bear it, my king. All of us. You can depend on us."

Another drawn-out moment of silence. Finally he nodded.

"Tell them to come with the bier."

"Yes, my lord."

Bathsheba turned around, wondering who she should call to carry out David's order. But a woman stood just behind her in the shadows.

"Did you hear?" asked Bathsheba.

The woman nodded. Was she one of David's wives? Or a servant? Or the wife of one of David's officers? Fortunately she didn't ask Bathsheba who she was and what she was doing there. Instead, she turned and walked down the hall.

Her mission complete, Bathsheba returned to the Assembly Hall, where she blended in with the mob of grieving courtiers who waited. No one had noticed her absence.

A short time later, David stepped into the room. Behind him four servants carried the bier with the body ready for burial.

Immediately a new wave of wailing swept the Assembly Hall. As the people glimpsed the white face on the bier, recalling her beauty, and how much they loved her, they shrieked and cried, fresh tears flowing down their cheeks. Already torn clothing was ripped even more.

Nathan stepped up and walked beside David. Together they plodded slowly before the bier, leading the grieving assembly out of the front gates. The men followed, and the women brought up the rear. A long procession weaved through the streets of Jerusalem to the Hinnom Valley just outside the Valley Gate, where the tomb had been prepared.

The noise reached a crescendo. All Jerusalem now joined their beloved king in mourning his favorite wife. And the din continued until David and Nathan and the servants disappeared into the tomb.

Then silence. Sudden, jarring silence. No one spoke. No one moved. The warm air was filled with the tension of grief.

When David emerged from the tomb, he stood tall and proud in the sunshine. A ray of the sun illumined his face, catching the fair hair and beard and turning it to a golden tint. His hair was actually brown, somewhat lighter than most Israelites. In the brilliant sunshine it sparkled, despite its lack of oil.

It was as though the finger of Yahweh had touched his face. His forehead was now smooth, and his lips seemed to be set in a straight line, not smiling, but not grimacing either. It seemed to Bathsheba — and probably to everyone else — that the David who emerged from the place of the dead had now returned to the place of the living.

The people dispersed silently toward their homes. No word would be spoken now until after sundown, and no food would be eaten. This was the time of mourning, when people remembered, when they shared silently the deep emotions of the bereaved.

As Bathsheba followed her husband home through the hushed Jerusalem streets filled with somber, silent mourners, her thoughts were on David. He had several wives and many sons and daughters. The royal household filled the huge palace the day they moved in.

But . . . who would occupy the big suite on the third floor? The Queen's Room. Who would sleep on that bed? Which of David's many wives would take Abigail's place?

Michal? The daughter of King Saul, whom David had married first? No. She was in disgrace. David never went to her bed.

Ahinoam? The second wife? A logical choice. The mother of Amnon, the heir to the throne. But she had no leadership ability and could never manage the complex household.

Maacah? Daughter of the king of Geshur? Her son Absalom was a handsome boy, whom many said would make a much better king than the sickly Amnon.

No one could begin to compare with the incomparable Abigail. Her death had left a void, a chasm, a bottomless pit, in the royal household.

Who would fill it?

Bathsheba sighed. If only. . . . But she shut off her thoughts as she plodded behind her stoic husband into the gates of their house. She mustn't think about that. She was a dutiful wife, married to Uriah. She would always be faithful to him. She could never be anything else.

2

The Philistines invaded Israel. Again. When Saul was king, they had invaded often. Sometimes they conquered Yahweh's people; sometimes they were beaten off. Always Israel survived, and life continued.

The Philistine rulers had believed that once King Saul was dead, the new king, David ben Jesse, would be their friend and ally. He had lived among them, and even marched to battle with them. But they soon discovered that David had no intention of allowing Israel to become a vassal state to the powerful Philistine nation. He asserted his independence early in his reign, claiming sovereignty, giving tribute to no one.

And so Philistia invaded.

The city of Jerusalem was stripped of its warriors, who went out to meet the Philistines. If defeated, there would be few fighting men left to defend the city. But they could still survive, because the walls were strong. Even a few could successfully repulse a powerful enemy. And a siege would last a long time.

Uriah had often mentioned to Bathsheba how well David had prepared Jerusalem for attack.

"He's the best military commander since Joshua," he once told her.

"Where did he learn that?" she asked.

Uriah shrugged, his muscular shoulders lifting the breastplate he almost always wore.

"He claims Yahweh taught him."

Bathsheba stifled the laugh which rose in her throat. Everybody knew about David's piety. They said it began when he was a shepherd boy, and God spoke to him while he tended his sheep. He was always singing a song he had composed himself, about Yahweh being his shepherd. She had never heard it, but everyone who did raved about its beauty and depth of religious feeling.

But who could believe Yahweh would teach the king about military tactics? That stretched credulity too far.

Bathsheba knew her husband Uriah believed in Yahweh only superficially. He had been born and raised in the north. His father was an officer in the Hittite army, and Uriah himself had trained as a soldier. His expertise was recognized by David, who hired him as one of his mercenary officers. When Uriah, recognizing that David's star was rising, committed his life and career to David, he submitted to circumcision and received his Israelite name of Uriah, which meant "the light of Yahweh."

Uriah believed not in God, but in war. In power. In military might. In sound tactics, good armor, fast horses, superior weaponry. War was his god, and he not only believed but worshiped this god.

Bathsheba saw nothing of her husband during the Philistine invasion. Even when he was home on leave, he stayed in the barracks by the palace. Bathsheba asked him once why he didn't come home when in Jerusalem.

"The war," he replied. "I cannot sleep in a comfortable bed with my wife while my men lie on pallets in the barracks or on the ground at the front."

She didn't miss him. Their love life was one-sided; he used her as an animal used its mate, for physical gratification. Her marriage to him had been commanded by David as a reward for loyal service. She must remain true to him because she was an Israelite woman, and all her training, all her culture spoke of loyalty to her spouse, even though there was no love in the marriage. She was content, however; as the wife of one of David's Mighty Thirty, she had access to the social life of the palace.

She took advantage of that now. Living next door to the palace meant that she could go every day if she wished to mingle with the constant crowd of courtiers in the Assembly Hall, even if the king and his men were absent.

That was where she became acquainted with Shua.

Shua was the wife of Hezro, one of David's Mighty Thirty. This made them social equals, and Bathsheba sought out Shua's company. Together they spent many hours in the palace, not just in the Assembly Hall, but in the back rooms where they mingled with David's eight wives and servants.

"I miss Mother Abigail," Shua told her.

Shua always called her *Mother* Abigail. Never Queen Abigail, her more common title. This reflected Shua's love for her queen. Shua had been Abigail's servant even before David had come into their lives, when her mistress had been married to that boor Nabal. Abigail had treated her not as a servant but as companion. Shua had been with her at her death.

"She loved the new palace." Shua wiped a tear from her cheek. "She spoke of nothing else during those last two weeks. It was everything she had dreamed it would be. And then . . . she died, after such a short time in her new home."

Bathsheba comforted her friend. As the days and weeks elapsed, they became close. Bathsheba felt she had in some small way replaced Abigail in Shua's affections.

The favorite place for the wives of David and his officers was the courtyard. The palace had been constructed in the northern style, following many of the magnificent building patterns of Tyre. Instead of being just inside the main gate of the house as in Canaanite architecture, the courtyard was in the center of the building, making it a private garden rather than a public foyer.

The palace courtyard was large, and the royal gardener tended it meticulously. Flowers and ferns and small shrubs grew among the stone benches. The grass underfoot felt soft and luxuriant, pleasant to walk on. The air was freshened constantly by the fragrance of flowers.

Here the women gathered to talk and enjoy the sunshine when the weather permitted. And here they kept abreast of the progress of the war against Philistia.

These women had one decided advantage over Bathsheba — their husbands talked to them. When they came home on leave from the battle, they spent the nights with their women, who then returned to the courtyard with fascinating tales of the campaign.

They told of the two battles of Rephaim. The Philistines had entered the long valley which led toward Jerusalem, and David had met them at a place of his own choosing. Repulsed, the enemy regrouped and came at them again.

"David asked Nathan the Prophet what to do," related Miriam, the wife of Shammah, one of the Mighty Three. "He of course asked my husband also, and Nathan miraculously confirmed Shammah's advice."

This brought knowing giggles from the wives. Miriam's husband Shammah was known as a braggart, and his jolly wife believed everything he said. David always consulted his professional military men when planning strategy, and Shammah, though notorious for bragging, was nevertheless respected for his intelligence and experience. Miriam carried her worship of Shammah even further, believing he knew more about military tactics than the prophet Nathan. Perhaps he did, mused Bathsheba, but Nathan was Yahweh's prophet, and Yahweh was Israel's true military commander, and David relied on Nathan for the final word.

"Our men sneaked around the Philistine army," continued Miriam, "through the Bechaim Woods, and came out directly behind them. They cut off their supply train. Then they attacked the Philistine rear guard from the forest. When the enemy turned on our men, they withdrew into the trees where the chariots couldn't follow. We beat them soundly."

"Any casualties?" asked Shua.

Her question was casual, but all the smiles disappeared as they awaited Miriam's answer. This was the question they had been waiting for. It changed the discussion from one of common gossip on the affairs of the day into something which could bring tragedy into the lives of one or several of these women.

Miriam smiled. "None. Our losses were extraordinarily light. Only a few fighting men. No officer."

"Yahweh be praised."

Bathsheba sensed the relief among the women and wished she shared it. How would *she* feel if Uriah were killed? She would never admit it — not even to herself — but the only loss she would experience would be these daily gossip sessions. She felt guilty about her lack of love for her husband, because she was a dutiful wife, and loyalty to Uriah demanded that she grieve sincerely if he died.

The war did not end with the successes in the Rephaim Valley. David led his army out against the Philistines, capturing the important city of Gath. Then swiftly he moved into the Sharon Plain and the Valley of Jezreel, conquering whatever Canaanite enclaves remained from the time of Joshua. Next he turned eastward, crossed the Jordan River, and attacked the Moabites, the Edomites, the Ammonites, and even the powerful Syrians. Wherever he went, he was successful. During several years of campaigning, the kingdom of Israel grew and consolidated.

Wherever the army of Israel went, the ark went with them. The ark of the covenant — that mysterious acacia wood box with the trumpeting cherub on it. Inside were the precious stone tablets of the Law, which, they said, were given to Moses by Yahweh himself.

The ark, carried by the priests, led the

men into battle. Some said it contained the presence of Yahweh himself. Others said no, God is everywhere; he doesn't live in a box. Nobody objected to using the ark this way, because it gave courage to the warriors and victory in battle.

David's successes were staggering. "From Dan to Beersheba" now meant a whole kingdom, unified, organized, powerful. David completed what Joshua had begun.

Finally peace came to Israel.

Peace — welcomed and cherished by the wives of the officers. Their husbands came home, thankful for the respite from battle, eager to renew their relationship with their wives and sire sons. The courtyard discussions became less strained, more cheerful, and very gossipy.

The gossip centered mostly on the power struggle among the wives of David. Constant bickering arose among them. Michal demanded more respect. Ahinoam flaunted her son Amnon, the heir to the throne, and Maacah boasted of her son Absalom, who grew in beauty and popularity as the years passed. "Just like his father," Maacah often said. More wives were added to the household, and the midwives were kept busy as more and more children were born in the palace.

But Uriah never came home.

He had been stationed at Rabbah, an Ammonite city which had somehow held out against the unrelenting tide of Israelite conquest. Uriah had become second-in-command, and his superior officer, Joab, could not spare him even to go home for a short leave. Uriah probably didn't care anyway. He would prefer to stay in the field where the battle raged, rather than return to Jerusalem and the luxury of his home and wife. Bathsheba shrugged. She didn't really miss him. But this feeling added to the guilt she already felt. Was she a dutiful wife when she felt that way?

She did see David more often, however. The prevailing courtyard gossip explained why. The king had come home to stay. Let his army do all the fighting for him. This was not due to David's lack of courage; no one doubted that. But something happened on the battlefield to change the long established policy that the king himself should lead his troops into battle.

Miriam herself told the story. Her husband Shammah had been on the battlefield when it happened. He had been badly shaken by the incident, and according to

Miriam his voice trembled when he told the story.

"The Philistines had this huge warrior," she told them. "Ishbi-benob was his name. He had a new suit of armor, and it reflected the sunlight. He was an impressive sight."

"How big was he?" asked one of the women. "As big as Goliath?"

Miriam nodded. "There were a lot of giants in the Philistine army. They're Anakim, and they come from Gath."

The Anakim! Giants descended from a race called the Nephilim, who in ancient times were so wicked they provoked Yahweh to send the Great Flood which destroyed everyone except the family of Noah. How the Anakim survived nobody knew, but Bathsheba suspected the stories about them were exaggerated. Mothers would scare their children when they misbehaved by saying, "The Anakim will get you if you don't watch out!"

When he was a boy in King Saul's army, David had killed one of these giants. Goliath. It had been recorded in the Sacred Story. But then, just recently Gath had been conquered by the Israelites, and the Philistines driven out. The Anakim giants among them, so they said, had fled to a small town called Gob. They now appeared occasionally as mercenaries in the armies of Israel's enemies.

The group of wives sat enthralled as Miriam continued her story.

"Shammah said it happened in a battle against the Ammonites in Trans-Jordan. David led a regiment of soldiers against a fortification. It went badly. The Ammonites were fierce! And they had some of those Anakim warriors among them. One had a spear big as a weaver's beam!"

Get on with your story, thought Bathsheba crossly. *What happened to David?*

Miriam smiled, enjoying the attention focused on her and her narrative.

"They flanked our men. Attacked from both sides. The center of our regiment collapsed. There stood the king, alone, with only a few men left, surrounded on all sides by enemies ready to snuff out the light of Israel!"

Just tell the story! thought Bathsheba again.

"That giant, Ishbi-benob, stood there in front of David, his new armor gleaming in the sun, and roared his challenge. 'Get back, everyone! I'm going to kill this little upstart king myself! Just watch me!'

"The Ammonite warriors backed off,

31

leaving the field to Ishbi-benob, who faced our king and just a few of our men. David swayed a little, showing his tiredness. It had been a long day of battle."

She's really dragging it out! thought Bathsheba.

"That was when Shammah came to his rescue! With the help of Abishai and a few others, he burst through the Ammonites and cut down the giant as though he were nothing but a twig on a tree. Shammah then fought off the other warriors, and Abishai led David back to our own lines. Abishai got all the credit, but Shammah was the one who really saved David's life."

Bathsheba knew the tendency of Shammah to tell stories about others and assign the heroics to himself. And Miriam was no better. What probably happened was that Abishai, the brother of Joab, had killed the giant, and Shammah had just been there as a minor participant. It didn't really matter, but Bathsheba wondered how this story would be related in the Sacred Story, or recorded in the Chronicles of the King.

Miriam wasn't through. "Shammah said to David, 'My lord king, we don't want you to fight any more battles. Why should we risk snuffing out the light of Israel?' "

"Snuffing out the light of Israel" was one of those dramatic phrases which Miriam, as well as her husband, Shammah, delighted in using. That part of the story Bathsheba believed; it sounded like something Shammah would say.

The story explained David's constant presence in the palace. Bathsheba saw him often. Most of the time he spent with his wives, especially his new brides. The number of sons and daughters born in the palace should increase in the months ahead.

Although David knew who Bathsheba was, and spoke to her casually in passing, he obviously did not remember the brief encounter in Abigail's bedroom on the day of her funeral. That was understandable; he had been ravaged by grief and probably recalled little of that tragic day.

From her own rooftop Bathsheba saw him occasionally on the roof of the palace. The palace was larger than her house, and from his high rooftop he sometimes looked down on hers. She had given up taking a bath on the rooftop. She would not miss her daily bath, even though now she had to take it inside her house.

3

Bathsheba's favorite time of year began with the *malkosh,* the last rain of the season. Now it was warm enough to spend more time on the rooftop.

She often strolled on her roof during these magical evenings, breathing deeply of the scented air. Flowers and green grass covered the ground, making the air delightful. Kings sent their armies out to make war in this season. Shepherds sheared their sheep and counted their newborn lambs. Farmers gloated over their crops. "They that sow in tears shall reap in joy," said the proverb with a double meaning.

And, so they said, it was a time for young lovers — animal or human — to seek their mates.

This delightful season of the year was suddenly cut off by a *sharav,* a week of oppressive heat. A dry east wind blew all day, bringing respite only at night. A dusty haze hung in the air. The flowers began to wilt, and the grass turned from bright green to sere yellow. The hot sun became the enemy. People sought the cooler interior of their houses during the day and relief on their rooftops at night.

Bathsheba looked forward to her nightly bath. She delighted in a clean body, and a bath in the cool night air brought refreshment to her spirit after a long hot day.

Tonight, she knew, would be a perfect time for a refreshing bath. It was the first full moon after Passover. The *sharav* was at its worst. All sensible people walked their rooftops these evenings. Hers had a parapet around it, high enough to afford privacy from surrounding houses.

Except for the palace, which loomed above her. But no one seemed to walk the palace roof at night. She wondered why. She suspected David had ordered it, but if so, why? And so many of David's household sought relief in the coolness of night by strolling in the courtyard; why not on the roof? But whatever the reason, since the palace roof was usually deserted, she decided she could tonight risk a bath outside after dark.

Bathsheba did not know — although she learned later — that the reason the palace roof was forbidden to the palace household was that David himself strolled the palace roof in the evenings. Alone. He needed time to himself to think, to plan, to pray, to compose his songs. So he decreed that the palace roof be deserted at night.

But unaware of David's need to stroll the rooftop, Bathsheba sought the cool night air for her bath. She waited until after midnight to ensure privacy and solitude. The night was still, the wind had died down, the air had cooled.

She awakened her handmaid. "Hephzibah. Prepare my bath."

"Yes, my lady."

"On the roof."

"The roof, my lady?"

The servant's face twisted in confusion. Hephzibah was only twelve years old; she had just recently matured. Her mother had been an Amalekite slave captured by David many years ago. Her father was an unknown Israelite warrior.

"The roof, Hephzibah. Now."

She understood her servant's confusion. For the past few years, her mistress had not taken a rooftop bath. Not since the completion of the palace. And never in the middle of the night.

"But . . . my lady —"

"Now."

Bathsheba walked away. The bewildered servant began heating the water on the cooking fire in the courtyard while Bathsheba chose her soap and perfume.

On the rooftop, Hephzibah had laid out the shallow bathtub and had already poured into it several buckets of warmed water. The soap, scented oil, and towels which Bathsheba had selected were laid out nearby.

The full moon was reflected in the bathwater. The air, still dry from the heat of the day, seemed fresher now, perhaps softened by the gentle moonlight.

Bathsheba lay in the scented water and closed her eyes. The warm water relaxed her. She felt the tensions of the day seeping out of her body. Now, with her eyes closed, all she wanted was to be left alone.

"Hephzibah," she murmured. "Leave me."

"My lady."

"Leave me."

"But —"

"Now."

"Yes, my lady," the servant whispered. She seemed to have a conspiratorial tone in her voice, although Bathsheba felt so relaxed she paid no attention. She listened as Hephzibah's footsteps scurried across the rooftop and down the steps to the courtyard.

Bathsheba proceeded with her bath, eyes closed, absorbing the peace of the night. After a long time, she rose from the tub and languidly dressed in a soft linen night-dress. She lay on the soft pallet which had been prepared for her on the roof.

She had just dropped off to sleep when she was startled by her servant's voice.

"My lady."

Hephzibah stood at the head of the steps. Bathsheba sleepily opened her eyes. She could see her servant's face twisted in a wry grin.

"Yes?"

"There is a man here. From the palace. He wants you to come with him."

"From the palace? But. . . ."

She was groggy from the relaxing bath and the beginning of sleep. Nothing made sense to her. Not the man from the palace, not the summons, not Hephzibah's knowing grin.

Bathsheba rose, donned a robe, and descended to the courtyard. The man stood in the moonlight, looking embarrassed. She recognized him as one of David's servants.

"My lady," he mumbled, trying not to

look at her. "Your presence is requested in the palace. It . . . it is the king's command."

She nodded and followed him out the gate. She was confused. But the king had commanded her presence and she must obey. And so she followed him.

No one was in the street. They hurried up the steps of the palace and through the large gate into the Assembly Hall.

"This way, my lady."

She followed mechanically down the darkened hall and climbed the stairway. She was reminded of another time a few years ago, when she had climbed these same steps. Only this time the servant led her past the large chamber on the third floor. They went directly to the roof, where the servant discreetly left her.

David stood there. The moonlight illumined his face, giving his hair and beard an almost golden tint. He was motionless. Embarrassed? No. Something else twisted his face. Lust.

She jerked fully awake. She knew why she had been summoned to the palace. She gasped.

"Be at ease, my lady."

The soft voice sounded strained. But it was the king's voice, and the king was her sovereign. Her mind swirled.

He took her into his arms. Gently. She felt she could do nothing but comply.

When she returned to her house a few hours later, a thunderstorm was breaking. The end of the *sharav,* no doubt. Bringing cooler weather. Delightful days lay ahead.

She sighed. Her mind was heavy with guilt. Not just guilt over the betrayal of her husband. Not just guilt that she, a woman of Israel, had committed adultery. Adultery was punishable by death, but she would have a powerful protector.

What disturbed her most was that the experience in the king's arms had been enjoyable.

Rain began to fall as she scurried through the courtyard and into her house, where a grinning Hephzibah awaited her. The *sharav* was over. She could look forward not only to better weather but more nights with the king.

The last words he had whispered to her just before she left the rooftop had given her as much joy as the time spent in his arms, even as they made the guilt flood through her.

"Come back again . . . tonight," he had commanded.

She would obey. Not just because he was

the king, and his word was law. She would obey because she wanted to.

Again the guilt rose. A storm of conflict twisted her soul. She had been untrue to her husband and committed adultery. And she had enjoyed it. She was falling in love with her seducer.

The days that followed were not as pleasant as the nights. The weather was fine, as warm moist air refurbished the landscape burdened by the *sharav*. But the air was unpleasant inside the palace.

Bathsheba tried to resume her place among the wives who frequented the palace courtyard. They shut her out. When she joined a group, they suddenly grew quiet, then one by one found other things to do. Even her best friend Shua refused to speak to her.

But the nights were delightful. Every night a cooling breeze blew, caressing her as she lay in her lover's arms on the palace roof. She had never known such ecstasy. She had never known a lover so considerate. Like so many women before her, she yielded to David's charms.

Bathsheba suspected that David had not given his love this fully to anyone since the death of Abigail. She was honored, her fantasies fulfilled. She had taken Abigail's place.

But David's bliss in their union was tempered by guilt. His guilt was as deep and disturbing as her own.

"We mustn't do this," he murmured to her one night. "It's against the law of Moses. It's not what Yahweh intended for his people. We are not goats, rutting in the mating season. We are humans, children of God who know better. We must stop."

She knew he was right. They should stop. But she trembled. If they did stop she would be devastated.

She breathed a sigh of relief when later, at the time for her to leave, he whispered, "Come tomorrow night."

One month later, the happiness abruptly ended.

"Hephzibah," she called to her servant one night when it was time to go to the palace.

"Yes, my lady?"

"Go to the king. Tell him . . . tell him I cannot come any more. I . . . I am with child."

She couldn't read the emotion on her servant's face, but she suspected it was a blend of amusement and smugness. Hephzibah said nothing, however, and went away on her errand.

So . . . this was Yahweh's punishment for

their sin. She would bear David's child. And of course, Uriah would know. What he would do, she did not know. Somehow he would punish her. Probably by death. She shrugged. She deserved nothing less.

And David?

His guilt matched her own. She could see it in his face. He was fighting battles deep inside, battles with himself, battles with Yahweh. What would he do?

Bathsheba heard no word from the palace. But surely David was planning something. He was the king, but even that could not prevent Uriah from taking revenge on her for her adultery. After all, the Law decreed that an adulteress must be punished by death. Death by stoning. She shuddered. Yahweh's Law was more powerful than the king's wishes. He could not protect her, and all she could hope for was that he could do something to prevent Uriah from finding out. But what? She waited.

A week later, her husband came home. So this was David's solution to the dilemma. The child to be born would be Uriah's. But if the baby had fair hair and a handsome face, wouldn't someone suspect? She shrugged. Everyone knew anyway. Who would be surprised? Uriah? But

43

he was always away, playing at war. Maybe no one would tell him. She snorted. A forlorn hope.

She steeled herself to accept the brutal lovemaking of her husband. After her experiences with David, it would be difficult indeed. But it had to be done.

After greeting her husband, washing his feet, serving him a meal, she was ready. But he put on his helmet and turned to leave.

"I'm going to the barracks," he growled, and left.

The next day he came home only for a few minutes. She wore a diaphanous robe and tried every allure she could think of to entice him to bed. Again he rose to leave.

"My husband," she said softly. "Please come to my bed. I need you. And it has been so long. . . ."

He shook his head. "I cannot, wife."

"But . . . why not?"

He stared at her, unfulfilled lust in his eyes. He set his mouth in a straight line. She could see the muscles in his jaw working.

"I can't. Not while the ark is in a tent at the front. And Joab and my men sleep on the ground."

He turned and stalked out, shoulders

slumped. The consummate soldier. More in love with war than his wife.

He didn't even come home the next day. She heard that he had returned to the front, bearing dispatches from the king to be delivered personally to Joab.

What she didn't know, and would not know until many months later, was the content of those dispatches. They were orders to make her a widow.

4

Two weeks later, they brought back to Jerusalem the body of Uriah the Hittite.

According to the gossip which floated around Jerusalem, related to Bathsheba by her handmaid Hephzibah, he was killed by arrows from the wall at Rabbah during a frontal assault. Joab's fault, the rumor said. He had ordered the futile attack, then failed to support it with reserves. It had been slaughter.

Bathsheba, wearing one of her old dresses, properly torn and covered with dust, waited for the return of her husband. Finally word came from the palace that the funeral procession had just entered the Valley Gate of Jerusalem. She was summoned for the burial.

The king stood on the palace steps with many of his officers. Everyone could see he was deeply moved. His fine robe had been torn in several places and covered with dust. His usually groomed beard and hair stuck out wildly, streaked with the mourning dust. His red-rimmed eyes stared vacantly. Tear streaks stained his dirty face.

Whispers floated around the mourners between cries and moans.

He hasn't mourned this much since Abigail's death.

Is this grief or guilt?

Will he make a speech today?

Bathsheba heard the whispers, even though they were drowned out by the wailing. And if she could hear them, wouldn't David hear them also?

He made no speech today, even though it was his custom to give a brief eulogy at the burial of one of his soldiers. A wise decision. Praise for his trusted lieutenant would be seen as open hypocrisy.

David led the procession as it plodded through the streets to the city gate, then out to the hillside where Uriah's tomb was located. He had purchased that tomb several years ago. All prominent families owned them, especially soldiers, who never knew when their lives would abruptly be cut off.

When they arrived at the tomb, David and a few of his officers entered the grotto to lay the body to its eternal rest. Grief silenced the waiting scene.

Bathsheba stood alone. All around her huddled the mourners, but even though she was the chief mourner, nobody came near her.

She had no one to comfort her. But then, she didn't need comfort. She squared her shoulders and held her head high and looked up into the skies. She didn't need anyone. Not now. Not ever. *Not even you, Yahweh.* This was how she determined to handle her guilt.

The next morning, a servant summoned her to the palace. He was not unexpected. The period of mourning had lasted until sundown last night, after which she had bathed. This morning she put on her best dress. When the call came, she and Hephzibah followed meekly to the palace.

The king sat on his great throne at the back of the Assembly Hall. Around him stood the familiar courtiers — the Mighty Men who were his military advisers, the statesmen, the priests, the advisers, including her grandfather Ahitophel. These men met here every day to discuss the affairs of the kingdom, make momentous decisions, initiate policies and programs, settle judicial cases. David, a wise king, did not hesitate to listen to and heed the counsel of his advisers.

Bathsheba took her place against the wall along with a few other women. Women were permitted in the Assembly Hall during these gatherings, although they were not allowed to speak or offer counsel.

The business of the kingdom droned on. A shepherd stood before the king, expressing a grievance. A wealthy land-owner nearby had stolen a lamb from his small flock. David's justice was adminis-tered, and the shepherd left the Hall a rich man. Ambassadors from Egypt were acknowledged; appropriate flowery words were exchanged. One captain was dis-patched to deal with a highwayman who terrorized travelers on the road from Jericho to Jerusalem. The usual business of the kingdom.

The next item of business came before them.

"Bathsheba." David's voice seemed loud in the suddenly hushed crowd of courtiers. "Come here."

Bathsheba pushed her way forward until she came to the foot of the dais. She caught a glimpse of several people on the platform, including that wild prophet Nathan. His unkempt appearance seemed out of place among the groomed courtiers.

His eyes blazed fiercely as he stared accusingly at her. With a guilty start she jerked her eyes away from him and turned to David.

"Yes, my lord king?"

David rose from his throne and came to her. He reached out his hand and took hers. He raised her to a place beside him on the dais.

"Bathsheba. Widow of Uriah the Hittite."

He looked around at the people gathered in the Hall, who now stood silent and embarrassed. Bathsheba bowed her head, suddenly ashamed.

"I now take you as my wife. So let it be done. Let it be recorded in the Chronicles of the King."

And that was all. She bowed before him, then stepped down and walked with as much dignity as she could manage to the doorway leading to the back hall. The only person in the assemblage who moved was Hephzibah, who followed her.

There was no one in the halls. Perhaps the palace people knew what had happened and went out of their way to avoid her. She didn't care. She walked proudly and with as much dignity as possible. When Hephzibah behind her let out a small giggle, she glared at her sternly.

Bathsheba climbed the stairs to the third floor. She knew exactly where she would go. The third floor. The Queen's Room. Now *her* room.

No one had occupied that room since Abigail's death several years before. It was up to David to decide which of his wives would move into it, thus becoming First Wife, leader of the household. He had never done this, and the family had been leaderless for the past few years.

She pushed her way into the room. It was hers now. David had not said so, but it didn't matter. She felt confident that he would not order her out.

She turned to Hephzibah and spoke sharply. "Go to our former home. Organize the move. Bring all my possessions. Now. And use the back door of the palace. Do not come in through the Assembly Hall."

Hephzibah grinned as she looked around at the luxuriously appointed suite. But she said nothing, other than an obedient "Yes, my lady," before scurrying out on her mission.

Bathsheba now stood alone in her new home. Abigail's room. No. Her room. She was the queen.

She stood before the window overlooking the courtyard three stories below. Women strolled there, chattering, gossiping. Talking about her, no doubt. Did they know that she had taken possession of the Queen's Room? Palace news traveled fast; surely they knew by now. What did they feel? Resentment? Anger? Hatred? Envy?

Bathsheba shrugged. She didn't care. She was queen of Israel now.

Queen in name only. She frowned. Not like Abigail. Abigail had been queen in every way. The people of the palace had looked to her for leadership. They had given her respect and even love. All Israel, in fact, had honored her. They had even called her "Queen Abigail."

They would never do that for Bathsheba. She was not Abigail. She was just another wife in the large household of wives and children who made up the growing family of the House of David. She would never be queen in anybody's mind but hers.

And David's. Yes, she would command a central place in her husband's affections. Above the others. He would love her as First Wife, even if she never had any authority over the household. That was the best she could hope for.

Or was there something else?

Yes. One more dream to be accomplished. She felt a grin break out and patted her belly. Maybe if she worked things right his child would be the next king of Israel!

Yahweh, is that possible? Will you help me do it?

The thought startled her. Not the thought that her unborn child might be the next king — but the fact that she prayed. She had decided to ignore Yahweh. That was how she would handle her guilt. But she knew she couldn't do that. She really did believe in him. She could not avoid that certainty.

David believed in him. Profoundly. He allowed his life to be ruled by his God. And burdened by guilt.

She stroked her belly again. This child — this boy — might be Yahweh's Anointed One. King of Israel. Her son. Only if Yahweh decreed.

Yahweh decree? He might. If she prayed, if she appeared pious, if she behaved properly, he just might decide to do so.

Then she would be the Queen Mother. The thought delighted her. She smiled. Yes. From now on, she would be a religious person.

Then why did fingers of guilt still probe her soul?

5

The weeks which followed were mixed ones for Bathsheba. Sometimes they were filled with rapture, other times with anger and loneliness.

The nights were the best. David came to the Queen's Room almost every evening, after the affairs of the day were completed. He came exhausted, often discouraged, occasionally angry, sometimes elated. And he would find peace and relaxation in her arms.

His need for her was not purely sexual. He would cling to her, as a child to his mother, seeking solace, security, and understanding.

She felt flattered. No, more than flattery inspired him to come to her. His custom was to sleep with one of his wives until she became pregnant. Then he would turn to another. But she was already with child; still he came to her. They said he had done this before. He had come to Abigail every night, even when other wives needed to be impregnated with the seed of the king, thus creating his dynasty. He had come to Abigail with love. And now, Bathsheba was sure, he came to her for the same reason.

Sometimes he sang for her. His soft melodious voice elicited from Bathsheba sighs of love, of joy, of peace. Although known for his skill in singing marching songs, stirring ballads of war, and rollicking tunes of ribald humor, he never sang those songs to her.

Many of his songs were psalms addressed to Yahweh. Sometimes, when political affairs were going well for him, the songs were bold statements of praise, offering thanks to the God who ruled Israel. Other times his psalm was a plea for help, expressing his own weakness and needs. Occasionally his song probed the deep pools of guilt in his life, pouring out to his God a wrenching need for forgiveness and love.

He sang the Shepherd Psalm for her, and she understood why everyone who heard it loved it. Bathsheba caught a glimpse into his soul, his need for the security and guidance of his Shepherd, his longing for still waters and quiet pastures, his lonely walk through the Valley of the

Shadow of Death. Ah, she sighed, if only she could believe in the Shepherd as David did!

When he made love to her, she discovered the secret an ingenious God had implanted in his human creatures when he made them male and female. Their clinging to each other was not merely gratification of sexual need, a clever way to ensure procreation and the continuance of the race. They also exchanged love through a profound encounter of two sensitive souls in a rapture more meaningful than just the momentary ecstasy of sexual fulfillment. Their two lives were brought together by love, by giving themselves completely to one another so that, as the Sacred Story put it so simply, "the two became one."

Because of the nights, Bathsheba was able to endure the days.

She felt outcast in her own home. The other wives shut her out. With the exception of her time with David, she was alone.

When she strolled in the courtyard, the wives of both the king and his officers turned from her. When she ate in the dining hall without men present, no one would sit with her. She tried to renew her friendship with Shua, but to no avail. Did her former friend blame her for the death of her husband in battle?

Compared with the nights, the days seemed long. Bathsheba sought diversion outside the palace. She commandeered a chair and some slaves and, with a small bodyguard, explored Jerusalem.

"The City of David," as people now called it, was truly a stronghold. The wall had been strengthened, especially in the north where it was most vulnerable, and the Jaffa Gate added. New construction loomed in the south and east, along the Hinnom Valley where it intersected with the Kidron Brook.

She saw the newly constructed home of David's son Absalom, rivaling in beauty if not size the palace itself. She passed the home of Amnon, the crown prince. And not far from the king's palace, she passed the large vacant lot reserved for the Temple, which would be built when Yahweh allowed its construction. But for now there was only a tent to house the sacred Ark of the Covenant when it was home rather than away leading Israel's army into battle.

The exploration of Jerusalem, although fascinating, could not completely absorb Bathsheba's restless energy. She wanted to be part of the palace society, to mingle with the wives, to be involved in the intrigue and gossip and struggles for power which made up the household. But a door had been slammed in her face.

Fortunately she had Hephzibah. Her handmaid worked her way into the lower echelons of palace society, mingling with the servants and slaves of the household. Bathsheba had no doubt her frivolous servant blabbed all her secrets, probably describing in lurid detail her trysts with David. She didn't care. If that was what it took to gain access to the palace secrets, it was worth it. Hephzibah brought back to her mistress all those secrets, and with great delight told every detail to Bathsheba.

She learned of the chaos the death of Queen Abigail had caused in the household. At first there was a power struggle to see who would take Abigail's place. No one succeeded. Nobody controlled anybody. Disputes were unresolved. Cliques developed; tempers flared. And there was no one to stop them.

Michal, oldest of David's wives, was known for her acid tongue and resentment. She was childless. Her bed had never been visited by David since she had returned to his household following an enforced separation. Nobody liked or befriended her, and she daily grew more shrill as she sank deeper into spinsterhood and old age.

Ahinoam, still clinging to her dark beauty and wasp-waist figure, meekly tried to ingratiate herself into the affections of her sister wives. They resented her because she was the mother of Amnon, the first-born son, the heir to the throne of David.

Maacah, proud princess from Geshur, got along with everybody, although she flaunted her children before the others. Her son and daughter had grown into beautiful maturity. Absalom, David's third son, was the exact image of David at that age, so everybody said. The same strong body, fair hair, bronzed face, winning smile. The charm. The magnetism. The ability to command love and respect.

And Tamar, his sister. So pretty. So soft. So likable. Everybody loved her.

Especially Amnon. The young heir to the throne of David could not hide his attraction to his half sister. Everybody saw this and giggled about it behind his back.

Now in their early twenties, the boys had chosen military service and were assigned as aides to the king. They could often be seen around the palace, hurrying about the business of the kingdom with a preoccupied air. Courtiers deferred to them, because they were the future of Israel.

Both Amnon and Absalom gloried in their newfound maturity and preoccupation with affairs of state. They became so busy they began to snub other members of the royal household, including their childhood companions. The handsome Absalom attracted the adoring attention of young women everywhere, and he responded. He built his own house in a fashionable section of Jerusalem, where he entertained with lavish parties and amorous trysts, generating gossip enough to fill the rooftops and courtyards of Jerusalem. Amnon, who had also built his own house, spent most of his time at the palace, where he continued to gaze with lovesick eyes at his half sister Tamar.

Bathsheba longed to be part of this royal household. She wanted to share in the joys and sorrows, the amusing incidents, the minor tragedies, the maneuvering for power, which were at the very heart of this family. Not even being David's favorite was enough to gain her entrance.

Daniel was the one exception.

Abigail's only son was David's second-born, and should have been in line for the throne of Israel if anything happened to Amnon. But he wasn't. An accident several years before had disqualified him.

Bathsheba recalled when it happened, because it was about the time she married Uriah. This was before the conquest of Jerusalem, when the royal family still lived in Hebron. Daniel was a young teenager, a strong, appealing youth, the pride of his mother, beloved of his father. He had entered military service and was military aide to Joab, the commander-in-chief.

On his first campaign, the boy had been struck down in a small skirmish by a sword thrust to the head. His helmet had saved his life, but the blow had damaged him severely. He never fully recovered.

Bathsheba saw him often in the palace, wandering around, affably joking with his siblings, talking seriously but meaninglessly with his aunts. Everyone loved him, pitied him, fawned over him. Sometimes his jaw sagged and spittle drooled over his chin. His eyes occasionally glazed over and stared vacantly. Although he could take care of himself, he could do only the most elemental things. His superbly developed man's body contained the mind of a child.

Once when Bathsheba rode in her chair into Jerusalem, she came across the youth wandering in the marketplace alone. She gave orders to stop the chair. Stepping down, she went to the boy.

"Daniel," she said.

The young man turned and stared at her. His eyes brightened as he recognized her, and a grin spread across his face.

"Mother Bathsheba!" he exclaimed, relief in his voice as well as on his face.

That he called her "Mother" was not surprising. Respectfully he called all women in the royal household that. He did not understand that this wife of David was not to be honored like the others.

"Where's Jubal?" asked Bathsheba, referring to the youth assigned him for companionship and protection.

Daniel shook his head, grinning. "I don't know, Mother Bathsheba. I think he's lost."

Bathsheba smiled. This young son of Abigail was likable not only because of his beauty but also because of his constant cheerfulness. His fear at being left alone in the marketplace had vanished with Bathsheba's appearance.

"Would you like to come back to the palace with me? I'll give you a ride in my chair."

Daniel's grin broadened; he clapped his

hands. "Yes! Oh, yes! Mother Bathsheba, that would be wonderful." Then his face clouded and he said, "But what about Jubal?"

"Don't worry about him, Daniel. He'll find his way home." And receive a good scolding when he arrived, no doubt, for deserting his charge like this.

Daniel scrambled into the chair and sat in front of Bathsheba. The slaves picked up the chair. Grumbling at the extra load, they set off through the streets toward the palace.

Bathsheba smiled fondly at the boy. "Does anybody ever call you Chileab?" she asked.

Daniel frowned and lowered his voice.

"Please don't call me that, Mother Bathsheba. Father doesn't like it."

Bathsheba nodded. Chileab was the name Abigail had given him. It meant "like his father." David had overruled her, saying he wanted no one to question the boy's parentage, since he had been born just nine months after his mother's marriage to David. Too many rumors floated around, saying this was really the son of Nabal, Abigail's first husband. So David had named him Daniel, meaning "God has judged," for reasons known only to David.

Bathsheba enjoyed talking with the boy, although she could not imagine why. It might have been her own loneliness; this was the only person in the palace society who was cordial to her. Or it might have been because she saw in the youth a reflection of David's image. Handsome, strong, fair — "like his father" indeed. No one would mistake him for Nabal.

During the weeks which followed, as her stomach swelled with new life, Bathsheba came more and more to appreciate the companionship of young Daniel. He eased the loneliness of the long days spent in the palace now that her pregnancy prevented her from going to the city.

Daniel came to her room often, which caused no small stir of gossip in the palace. Except for his mind he was a mature man, and speculation among the gossips about what happened in that room were not quelled even by Hephzibah's repeated declaration of Bathsheba's innocence.

Bathsheba's delight in her situation was tempered by guilt. She could not deny the reality of God's judgment. Somehow she felt responsible for David's great sin. Even though she had been unaware of David's presence on the palace roof above her, she felt she had tempted David by taking a bath where he could see. Her servant might have been trying to warn her of David's presence, but she had not listened. She felt she must at least share David's guilt.

She had tried to ignore Yahweh. But she could not deny God. When she listened to David singing his songs at night, she felt the same closeness to God her husband obviously felt. And when David sang of his guilt feelings, they became her feelings too. Her happiness with her new husband mixed with feelings of disloyalty to her first husband, whose innocent life had been snatched from him because of their sin. She and David were both guilty before Yahweh, and deep within she felt the agony of this guilt.

Or so she thought — until the day the prophet Nathan pushed his way into her life.

6

Sometimes, to relieve the boredom of the long days, Bathsheba would slip unnoticed into the Assembly Hall to listen to the affairs of the kingdom. She wore a veil and a loose robe; it was unseemly for an obviously pregnant woman to appear boldly in public.

David dispensed justice and administered political affairs with a confident air. Ambassadors from surrounding nations, large and small, came before him, to exchange compliments and assurances of peace and continued trade. Messengers from Joab reported the continuing siege of Rabbah, and David sent back words of encouragement and advice. He initiated building projects, improved roads, established trade agreements with nations near and far, and commissioned a navy on the Great Sea. And always justice was dispensed — fairly, rapidly, wisely.

Bathsheba huddled in an inconspicuous corner as these historic events unfolded. She watched fascinated, always marveling at her husband's skill and wisdom. She especially enjoyed his decisions in judicial matters. He did not favor the rich; instead he meted out justice to all.

Often requests for the king's justice were brought before him by the prophet Nathan, who seemed constantly to champion the cause of the poor in the land. He stood before the dais now.

"O king, live forever!"

Formula words, spoken by everyone who addressed the sovereign. Nathan's confident, well-modulated voice could be heard by all in that hushed hall. Bathsheba felt tension rise in the crowd of courtiers.

"Two men live in this city. A rich man. A poor man."

Bathsheba had heard Nathan present his stories before and knew what was coming. A request for justice.

"The rich man has a large flock of sheep. Many flocks, in fact, and a herd of goats. The poor man has nothing. Nothing except a small ewe lamb."

Bathsheba, like all in the Assembly Hall, marveled at Nathan's skill. He often began the presentation of his cases with a parable.

"This lamb was the children's pet. He fed it at his own table. It drank from his cup. At night he let it sleep in his own bed. It was like his own daughter."

Suddenly, Bathsheba felt a hand of ice grip her heart.

Like his own daughter. The word was *batseba.* Almost her own name. The icy hand gripped more tightly.

"Then came a traveler to the rich man's home. He prepared to entertain his visitor but did not take a sheep from his own flock for dinner. Instead, he took the poor man's lamb. He killed it, roasted it, and served it for dinner."

Bathsheba knew exactly what the parable meant.

David obviously did not. He rose to his feet, face dark, brows drawn together. "I swear by Yahweh the living God," he thundered, "that man shall die! First, however, he shall restore to the poor man fourfold what he has taken from him. He — he —"

Words failed him. His face was red; his eyes blazed. Everyone knew David's reputation for justice.

Then came a moment of silence. In that dramatic moment, Nathan leveled his finger at David. "*You* are that man!"

A mighty gasp rose from the crowd. David's face turned pale, and he sank back on his throne. He knew now what

Nathan's parable meant. And so did all the people in the Assembly Hall.

Including Bathsheba. Her throat constricted. Her stomach tightened. Pain shot through her abdomen.

She stumbled out of the hall, down the corridor, into the courtyard. She sat on a bench, gasping for breath. Fortunately nobody was in the courtyard.

A moment later, David and Nathan strode into the courtyard. They did not notice her.

David's voice sounded strained and weak. "What did you mean by all that?"

Bathsheba could hear them plainly. She bit her lip. David knew exactly what Nathan meant.

Nathan's voice, which had seemed booming in the Assembly Hall, now sounded soft and compassionate. "Thus says Yahweh: 'I made you king of Israel, and delivered you from the power of King Saul. I gave you two kingdoms, this palace, many wives. And there was more to come! But you have despised my laws and defied me. Therefore, my lord king, tragedy shall follow. Your own household shall rebel against you. Many of your sons will die and your wives be violated. What you did, you did in secret; what happens next will be open for all to see!' "

David buried his head in his hands and sank to his knees. He tore his robe. "I have sinned against Yahweh. I deserve to die."

So much anguish poured out of David that Bathsheba's heart went out to him. He had spoken often and composed songs about the deep pool of guilt within him. Now it came wrenching out in tears and moans.

Nathan's hand reached out and touched his head. His words were gentle. "You shall not die. But . . . your child will."

A sharp pain racked Bathsheba's body. She cried out. The two men in the court-yard turned to her, seeing her for the first time. They came to her as she writhed in pain on the bench.

Events happened swiftly. Servants were summoned. They carried her to her room. Midwives came and attended her. The child was born in pain and sorrow.

A boy.

The baby was sick. Bathsheba knew it immediately. She was not surprised. The child had been cursed by Yahweh.

The infant would not nurse at her breast. His cries grew weaker with each passing day. For seven days. Then he died.

During that week, Bathsheba saw nothing of David. She tried to bear her suffering, although she suffered alone. She learned from Hephzibah that David mourned in the courtyard, in the open air, spending days and nights on the bare ground, refusing food. No one could comfort him.

Nor could anyone comfort Bathsheba. The wives would not draw near her. Hephzibah tended her physical needs but could offer no comfort. Not even her friend Daniel could find the right words to say to her.

When the baby died, Bathsheba sat on the floor beside the bed where the body lay. She stared at it. So small. So white. So wizened from illness. So . . . cursed by Yahweh.

Yahweh! The God of love and compassion. She shook her head slowly as she gazed at the lifeless body. This God had no love or tenderness in him. Not for her, anyway.

Nor for David. Yahweh's beloved, they had called the king. Ha! Yahweh's cursed one, more likely.

This was the punishment for their sin. This was how Yahweh took his revenge on two people who had the audacity to defy the Law of God. Revenge! Was that what

God had done to them? Not only them. Yahweh had just murdered an innocent child. She shuddered. How could she believe in such a God? This was no God of love. He was a God of vengeance, punishing innocent people who disobeyed his Law. He was just like Chemosh and Dagon and Moloch and all those other so-called false gods.

She didn't know how long she sat there, staring vacantly at the dead child, wondering about the God who ruled their lives so sternly.

David walked in. She looked up at him, startled. He looked magnificent! He had on new clothes. His hair and beard were oiled and combed, his body smelled fresh and clean from his bath, and he was smiling.

"Come, wife," he said tenderly, reaching out his hand to her. "Bathe yourself. Get dressed. We must lay the child in his tomb."

She stared at him, her mouth open.

"I don't understand. How can you. . . ."

He took her in his arms and kissed her forehead.

"Why must we grieve when he is dead?" he murmured. "Will our sorrow bring him back? No. Some day we shall go to him, but he cannot come back to us."

Bathsheba responded to his gentleness. David held a power over her. She had always been able to match him mood for mood. She did so now. And she recovered.

She recovered in body, but not in soul. She experienced the love of her husband, but not the love of God. That love had been denied her.

But had she ever had it? Only vicariously. Through David. He was Yahweh's beloved, and this love overflowed to her. But it had never really touched her personally. Only peripherally. When it touched David, it touched her. But David's God had not entered her life.

Desperately she wanted to feel that touch.

7

Life in the palace went on as before. David spent his nights with Bathsheba, desperately seeking solace and refuge in their love. He continued to be optimistic in spite of his feelings of guilt.

"Yahweh is good," he told her one night. "He has punished us for our sin, and now he will forgive us. You'll see."

Bathsheba was reluctant to believe him, even when she discovered she had become pregnant for the second time.

"Strange," she said thoughtfully, "I have always believed in God. He was once an important part of my life. He was kind and loving. But no more. I cannot accept him as good and forgiving and kind to me. Why is that?"

David shrugged. "I don't pretend to understand the mind of God. I only know what he has done for me. And God is good."

"You are Yahweh's Anointed. That is why he is so good to you. But he pays no attention to me. How can I know he is good to me for myself, and not just because I'm married to you?"

"Not even if you give birth to another son?"

"And how do I know Yahweh won't do to our next child what he did to our first?"

Her question startled David. For a long moment he sat in silence, rubbing his chin with his thumb and forefinger. Finally he spoke in a soft voice.

"He has punished us once. And forgiven us. How can we believe he will continue to curse us for past sins? We have repented. Can't we believe that now he will bring us good to balance the punishment?"

Bathsheba didn't reply. David said nothing more. She felt sure David did not fully believe what he had just said. Did he think God's punishment was over? She shrugged. The subject was beyond their understanding; they could not penetrate the depths of the divine mind.

Nevertheless, Bathsheba had dark thoughts about their future. Yahweh was now real to her, but he was a God who kept his promises — and threats. Nathan, who spoke for him, had predicted their first child would die in a week, and he did. What else had Nathan foretold? Rebellion in the royal family, death of some of David's sons, rape of David's wives. She shuddered. Her husband did not speak of these things. Nor did she. They were better left forgotten.

Word came from Joab at the front. The water supply of Rabbah had been taken, and the city would fall in a short time. Joab invited the king himself to come to Rabbah and take credit for the victory. If David did not come, the city would probably be called the "City of Joab," just as Jerusalem was called "City of David" — and Joab refused this honor. It was typical of David's commander-in-chief; his devotion to his sovereign reached far beyond his own need for glory and recognition.

And so David went off to battle, even though his advisers had warned him against placing himself in danger. David confided in Bathsheba that he must be there in person at the end, for a more important reason than to receive credit for the victory. His wisdom and statecraft were needed to supervise the distribution of wealth and slaves from the captured city. The nation of Israel must profit after so long and costly a siege, and the decisions which followed would be more than the warrior Joab could handle.

David's absence lasted for several months, and Bathsheba missed him greatly. Much to the dismay of the gossipy wives in the palace, she spent much time in the company of young Daniel. But Bathsheba found another friend. . . .

She rose early each morning to walk in the courtyard. This was a golden time of day for her. None of the other women were awake yet, and she cherished the time she spent alone in the garden. The fresh morning air was invigorating, and the light dew on the grass and flowers sparkled in the sunlight. She discovered she could be more optimistic at this time and in this environment than at any other time of day.

Then Nathan the prophet joined her. Perhaps he had found her accidentally, but she suspected he had heard of her daily habit and sought her out. Nathan's usually stern demeanor softened in this peaceful setting, and he became almost human. He spoke quietly and in a soothing tone. He was quite different from the forbidding prophet of Yahweh who often thundered his judgments in the Assembly Hall.

"Yahweh be with you, my child."

He greeted her this way each morning. No recriminations. No disapproval. No pronouncements of divine judgments upon her. Just gentleness and cordial respect.

They spoke of David, of the victory at Rabbah, of the new wave of road building and house construction resulting from the wealth and slaves taken from Rabbah. They spoke of David's wisdom, his faithfulness to Yahweh, his charm in dealing with people. This prophet, who looked like a wild man from the desert, became for Bathsheba a loving father-figure, and she grew to love him.

One morning, after several weeks of daily companionship, she felt she knew him well enough to ask a bold question. "Does God really speak to you?"

He smiled at her. "Yes, my child. He does. Really."

"How?"

He shrugged. "I don't know. Not by an actual voice. Just . . . an awareness in me."

His civility encouraged her to plunge on. "But how do you know it's really Yahweh's voice? Isn't it just your own thoughts and ideas, which you piously ascribe to God?"

She thought she had offended him, but he merely smiled and answered her. "I have wondered that myself. But always I discover that the messages he gives me are far beyond anything my feeble mind can conceive. Sometimes they are predictions of the future. And they always come true. Yahweh has never been wrong yet. If they were merely my ideas, they would be guesses. And they would often be wrong. But they are always right. So I know they come from Yahweh."

She nodded. "I guess he speaks to David also. It must be nice to have a God who speaks to you."

"He's your God too, my child."

That was where their discussion ended, as it so often did on these intimate mornings. Somehow she had closed the door on probes into her own personal feelings.

Day after day they walked together, sharing thoughts. The moments became precious to her, and she looked forward to their tryst each morning.

As the weeks passed, her belly again swelled with new life.

Nathan spoke of it one morning. "Your son is strong," he said.

"My son? How do you know it's — oh. Did God tell you that?"

He nodded. "I feel certain he will be strong and wise."

"And healthy?"

The prophet stopped in his walk and turned to her. His eyes bored into hers.

"You still resent Yahweh's punishment, don't you?"

Bathsheba had paused when he stopped, but now she turned and continued walking. He followed.

They could talk about anything at all — David, the kingdom, Nathan's insights into the nature of God, even her unborn child — but when he reached into her personal thoughts, she walked away.

This time, however, he pursued her. "God loves you, my child."

She said nothing. She continued walking.

"And your son will become the next king of Israel."

She stopped, gasping. What he said was impossible. Preposterous. Slowly she turned to face him. "No. No. I want nothing like that for me or my son. Nothing but trouble comes to him who wears the crown. Just tell Yahweh to leave us alone."

He shook his head slowly, and his next words were gentle. "We can't tell Yahweh what he must or must not do. But just remember this, my child. He loves you . . . and your son."

She turned away. She could not believe him. She *would* not believe him. It *couldn't* be true. It couldn't! All the misery and trauma and tragedy which Yahweh had ordained for David's future must not touch her or her son.

She could believe in Nathan and David's Yahweh, but she could not accept his love.

The next morning the prophet confronted her. "You must love God, my child. For he loves you."

Again she turned away.

But he pursued her, speaking gently. "Your guilt is misplaced. God is not angry with you."

She sighed, and turned to face him. "Not angry with me? After killing my child and threatening dire consequences for David's family? How can you say that?"

"Yahweh is a God of justice, Bathsheba. He is not punishing for reasons of revenge. That is the difference between chastisement and punishment. Punishment is for revenge; chastisement is to teach, to develop character."

Bathsheba said nothing. Her mind seethed with confusion. These were old lessons, and the prophet sounded pedantic, like an old teacher going over stale truths.

Bathsheba stared at the ground. Perhaps if she retreated into silence, Nathan would leave her alone.

But he would not. He pressed on. "I have said your guilt is misplaced. God is not chastising you. His justice is directed only at David."

She could hardly believe this. Their sin was a joint one; they were equally guilty.

Almost as though he read her thoughts, Nathan continued. "It was David's sin, not yours. You did not seduce him. You were innocent. The king commanded. You obeyed."

She shook her head but said nothing. What he said was difficult to believe. She still felt guilt. How could it not be her fault?

The prophet continued. "Your guilt stems from the love you have for David. You feel disloyal to your first husband, whom you never loved. As a result of David's great sin, you were forced to commit adultery, and as a result you fell in love with David. That is why you feel guilt."

Bathsheba could not absorb this. What he said might be true. But it was too much to accept now. Perhaps later.

"You need not feel guilty about loving David. Yahweh has set his seal of approval on love within marriage. You are God's child. Accept that. Accept his love for you.

If you do, you will find peace in your soul."

Still Bathsheba said nothing. Maybe later she would accept what Nathan was telling her. That God loved her. That he did not disapprove of her love for David. That she had no reason to feel guilty, or disloyal to her first husband, or that God had cursed her. Maybe later. For now she just stood stunned, staring at the ground.

Perhaps understanding and respecting her silence, Nathan walked away, leaving her to her thoughts. But she could not force her mind to think about anything. Not today. Tomorrow . . . maybe.

David returned from the city of Rabbah in time for the birth of their child. The time came and the midwives were summoned. As predicted, the infant was a boy. A strong, healthy boy.

David himself placed the child on Bathsheba's knees in the centuries-old tradition for naming children. "His name is Solomon," he said solemnly.

"His name is Solomon," echoed Bathsheba.

A good name. It meant "God is his peace." Only one other son of David had the root word for peace in the name: Absalom, meaning "his father's peace."

Bathsheba wondered if there were any-thing significant about that. One child was named for the peace of his father; the other for the peace of God. Would the one named for the peace of his father have the same kind of peace in his life his father had? And would the other have the kind of peace God gave?

She shrugged. Such thoughts were far-fetched and not very practical. It was more practical to compare young Solomon's name to Jerusalem. The name of the city meant "foundation of peace." Was there anything significant about the boy named "God is his peace" and the city named "foundation of peace?" No. No. These were just names. Nothing more.

A few days later, she brought the child to the courtyard in the early morning. She had heard that Nathan walked there every day at their usual time, perhaps waiting for her to recover from childbirth and resume their walks. She was eager to show her friend her baby.

Nathan's hard face softened as he saw the child. He took him into his arms, smiling. "His name is Jedediah," he mur-mured.

"No," replied Bathsheba. "We've already named him. Solomon. The king has so decreed, and he has already ordered it written in the Chronicles of the King."

Nathan shook his head slowly. "No," he said softly. "His name is Jedediah. Yahweh has so decreed."

Bathsheba looked at her mentor wistfully. "I wish it were so. I like your name better. Will you ask David to change it?"

"No." Nathan shook his head of unruly hair. "No, let it stand. Solomon shall become a name known to all the world. Jedediah will be just for you."

The name filled Bathsheba's heart with warmth. It meant "beloved by Yahweh." A good name.

And if Yahweh loved this child, could he not love his mother also? Perhaps the private name Nathan had given her child was the one thing she needed to accept God's love for her.

8

Bathsheba decided her life in the palace as the king's favorite wife was not a lonely one, in spite of the way the other wives treated her. She now had four companions to banish the loneliness.

David. His love for her was genuine and profound. He came to her every night after his duties were completed. He had younger concubines constantly presented to him by Israelite fathers in hopes of receiving favors in return, but David visited their beds only sporadically. He sometimes impregnated them with the royal seed, then abandoned them. If he did not impregnate them, he abandoned them anyway. It was as though his love for his wife was more important than the sexual attraction of youth and beauty.

Daniel. David's feeble-minded son spent a lot of time with Bathsheba. He became an uncle to the child Solomon, and tended him, played with him, talked to him at every opportunity.

Solomon. The baby absorbed her life now. She discovered the joys of motherhood as well as the difficulties. Sometimes her chores were boring. Often she dragged through the days exhausted after an active night at her child's bedside, and occasionally his continued crying with colic or teething almost drove her mad. But like all mothers, she found that when she coaxed a smile and a giggle from the baby, that one precious moment canceled out the frustrations, weariness, and boredom of motherhood.

Nathan. The prophet continued to seek her out in the courtyard, and their walks brought comfort and new insights to Bathsheba. She began to realize that not only the prophet's words but also his love for her were leading to her acceptance of God's love. Strange, that God's love can be communicated through a person's actions even more clearly than through the words.

Four companions. She decided she was no longer lonely.

Although the servant was apparently loyal to her, she could not count her handmaid Hephzibah as a companion. She was a flighty girl, absorbed in hearing and tattling the gossip of the palace. That she kept Bathsheba informed, Bathsheba could not deny. But the price of this palace espionage was that Hephzibah spread the gossip of the royal bedchamber through the palace. Everyone in the household knew as much about her as she knew about them.

It was through Hephzibah that Bathsheba learned about Amnon and the infatuation that young man had for his half sister Tamar.

"That boy." Hephzibah rolled the words around on her tongue, thoroughly enjoying the telling of her tale. "He spends more time at the palace than at his own house. He doesn't even keep concubines at his house. He can hardly do the duties his father assigns to him. All he does is follow Tamar, making moonstruck eyes at her."

That topic of gossip traveled around the palace network, providing whispers and giggles to the servants. They found the adventures of their masters and mistresses a source of delightful entertainment.

"And how does Tamar feel about him?" asked Bathsheba, only mildly interested. "Or more important, how does her brother Absalom feel?"

"Oh, Absalom doesn't care. He pays more attention to the girls he keeps at his house than to his own sister. Tamar? Well

. . . I think she likes the attention. It's something to keep her mind occupied while she waits for the king to decide her future."

Bathsheba nodded. David needed to find a husband for the beautiful Tamar. Just one more decision for the king. He had several daughters who would be sent to foreign capitals for marriage to young princes. The daughters of the powerful King David were in great demand these days.

Then one day Hephzibah brought Bathsheba an item of gossip which startled her.

"That young man —" Hephzibah said snippily "— he did it. He just went and did it."

"Who?" demanded Bathsheba. "And did what?"

"Amnon. He raped Tamar. And him the crown prince, too!"

Bathsheba gasped. Amnon's youthful infatuation for his half sister was treated with amused tolerance by everyone in the royal household and indeed all Jerusalem. But until now it had seemed harmless.

Hephzibah knew the story in detail, as she did all the stories circulating in the kitchens and bedchambers of the palace.

This one had happened only a few hours ago.

Amnon had taken to his bed at his house. Sick, he said. "Lovesick, more like it," sniffed Hephzibah. He had asked his father to have Tamar bake a loaf of honey bread for him.

She had come to his house, alone except for a servant named Hannah. The princess couldn't help but know of her brother's infatuation but responded only as a sister fond of a doting brother. She went into his bedroom where he lay and prepared bread in his presence.

"Hannah said she knew something was up when that boy ordered all the servants to leave the bedroom and shut the door," Hephzibah continued. "Pretty stupid of the princess, I'd say."

Not many mistresses allowed their servants to speak as Hephzibah did. But Bathsheba tolerated it, because her hand-maid was a mine of information. She enjoyed telling her story, and she told it now with relish.

"When she handed him the fresh-baked bread, he grabbed her arm. Huh. She finally caught on to what he was up to."

Hephzibah then described the rest of the story with exaggeration and graphic details. Tamar had pleaded with Amnon not to do it. She was a virgin, destined for a political marriage. This thoughtless act would soil her life forever. But nothing could stop Amnon.

"When it was over," said Hephzibah, almost smacking her lips with delight, "the prince kicked her out. Had his servant throw her out the door. Bodily. And then lock the door behind her. Hee, hee!"

Bathsheba could see nothing funny about the incident. Incident, no — it was a family tragedy!

"Has the king heard about this?" she demanded.

"Oh, no. Nobody tells him anything!"

This was certainly true. But the king must know. What he would do about it, Bathsheba had no idea. But he must know.

"Where is Tamar now?" she asked her servant.

Hephzibah shrugged. "I don't know. She's not in the palace. Maybe she went to her brother's house."

That made sense. Absalom's house was not far from Amnon's. Absalom wasn't home, however. He was at Rabbah just now, distributing the spoils of war. Good thing. What that impetuous young man

91

would do if he were here was not good to think about.

Bathsheba told her husband that night when he came to her room. He had not known. By now everybody in Jerusalem knew, except David.

The king took it badly. He paced the floor, tearing his clothes, shaking his head, occasionally stopping to stamp his foot on the floor.

"That fool!" he muttered. "That stupid, lovesick fool! Doesn't he know what could happen? When Absalom hears about this —"

"He'll hear soon enough," said Bathsheba. "Maybe you'd better talk to him as soon as possible."

David paused in his pacing, his thumb and forefinger stroking his chin.

"Yes. You're right. But how can I? He's in Rabbah now and I can't go to him. Well — maybe he'll cool down after a while."

"I doubt it." Bathsheba went to him and touched his hand. "Is this the beginning of Nathan's prophesy?"

A wince of anguish crossed his brow. "I fear so. Yahweh is still angry with me for my sin. When will it end?"

Yet the matter seemed to have ended there. Absalom didn't come home immediately, but when he did, he said nothing. David left it at that. Bathsheba wondered if the hotheaded youth would just pass it off and seek no revenge. Unlikely. But nothing happened and the incident seemed forgotten, except for the delighted wagging of tongues at the lower levels of Jerusalem society over the troubles of the royalty.

The months passed. Except for a coolness between the brothers Absalom and Amnon, the incident was left behind. Beautiful Tamar was forgotten. She now lived in Absalom's house, in virtual spinsterhood. Her life had been ruined by her half brother, and that young man, now relieved of his infatuation, didn't seem to care.

Had Absalom really forgotten? Bathsheba doubted it. He saw his sister every day at his house. Her sorrow and loneliness reminded him constantly. Amnon's indifference and haughtiness must be fueling the fires of inevitable tragedy.

But in the palace, Bathsheba continued her serene life. Solomon grew, took his first toddling steps, and marched into the hearts of all who saw him. Daniel adopted him, and they were seen walking hand-in-hand all over the palace. The boy, reflecting the inherited characteristics of his father, charmed everyone he met.

Two years after the rape of Tamar, word came to the palace of tragedy. David's sons — all of them — were in the town of Baalhazor, just twelve miles northwest of Jerusalem. Absalom had developed a sheep ranch there, and he had invited his brothers for a sheep-shearing festival.

Bathsheba was among the courtiers in the Assembly Hall when a messenger arrived.

"They're dead!" screamed the young man as he burst through the throng of courtiers assembled around David. He hadn't bothered with the courteous "O King, live forever" which was the usual greeting to the sovereign.

"Who's dead?" demanded David.

"Your sons, my lord. Absalom murdered them!"

"What?" David leaped to his feet. "What are you saying?"

"It's true, my king. I saw it. They were celebrating the sheep-shearing festival. All of a sudden, Prince Absalom's men surrounded them and began shooting arrows at them. They're all dead!"

"No, no, it can't be!"

But then David sank to his knees and

tore his robe. Ever since Nathan's prediction, he had expected trouble in his family.

Tears burst from Bathsheba's eyes as she heard the news. All of David's sons! David had twenty-seven sons at the time, all born either of wives or concubines. That included young Daniel, the son of Queen Abigail, but fortunately not Solomon. The three-year-old had been too young to go and had remained at the palace.

And Amnon! The crown prince, whom Absalom hated. Absalom's hatred had been smoldering for two years and now had erupted in fury. But to kill all his brothers!

"My lord king!" A strong voice sounded in the Assembly Hall among the agitated voices of courtiers who followed the king's lead and sorrowed.

The voice belonged to one of David's counselors. One with a cooler head. He spoke boldly now. "This can't be true, my lord king. Absalom would not kill them all. Amnon, maybe. Everybody knows how he felt about the crown prince. But not all his brothers! Check this report out, my king, before you mourn."

Another messenger arrived at that moment. A soldier, still wearing his helmet and breastplate. One of the guards at the north gate of Jerusalem. "Someone's coming, my lord king. From the north. I saw a cloud of dust and several riders on mule-back approaching!"

The king and his courtiers hurried out of the palace to the northwest gate of the city. Bathsheba went to the palace roof. In the distance she could see them approaching. The riders on mule-back were not an army. There were no soldiers among them. Some were young, merely boys.

Then Bathsheba knew who they were. David's sons. The story was not true then! But something tragic had obviously happened.

Later Daniel himself brought the story to her. "We were at the sheep festival," he reported. "And Absalom told his men to kill Amnon! They did. They shot arrows into him. Oh, it was horrible!"

Bathsheba comforted the young man as best she could, but it was Solomon who finally enabled Daniel to stop his tears. "Dan'l," he lisped. "Don't cry."

Bathsheba herself could not keep back the tears. *It has begun,* she thought. The tragedy of Nathan's prophecy. *Where will it end?*

9

Absalom was gone. Fear of his father's wrath had driven him into exile. Word came to Jerusalem that he had found refuge in the nation of Geshur across the Jordan River. His mother, the princess Maacah, had come from there. The old king Talmai still lived and ruled the tiny nation, and he gladly offered a home to his grandson.

David longed to see his handsome son. He would not speak of it publicly, but at night when he came to Bathsheba after a busy day, he told her of his love for his son.

"Absalom is still my son," he said. "My beloved son. He has nothing to fear from me. If he would only come home, I would forgive him, and everything would be as before."

But Absalom did not come home.

One night David told Bathsheba, "Joab wants me to send word to Geshur and bring Absalom home."

"Joab?" Bathsheba frowned. "Why does he want that?"

David shrugged. "Who knows, with Joab."

"Don't trust him."

"That's what everybody tells me. But Joab has always been loyal to me. Sometimes he acts in strange ways, but always what he does is for my benefit. I feel sure he would not desert me and go over to Absalom."

Bathsheba shuddered. Despite his wisdom, her husband was so naive sometimes. She looked at him. Streaks of gray had invaded his hair and beard. Years and responsibilities had engraved deep lines on his face. A puffiness had appeared on his body, showing lack of exercise.

Yet in many ways he retained the vigor and energy of a man half his age. His active mind was filled with new ideas, new projects, new ways of improving his kingdom. Now in his fifties, wisdom gleaned from a lifetime of experience gave him an aura of dignity absent in his youth.

Bathsheba recalled Absalom, now in his early thirties. An exceptionally handsome youth. He had the same fair hair, piercing eyes, regal bearing, and smooth facial skin which had characterized David in his youth. And the charm. Everybody loved this man they believed next in line for the throne. Few regretted the loss of Amnon, not nearly as regal or attractive as Absalom.

"Why don't you bring him back?" asked Bathsheba.

David rubbed his chin. "I don't want anybody to think I approve his murder of Amnon."

Bathsheba nodded. David had always maintained that no one should harm Yahweh's Anointed — or anyone in the royal family. Regicide. A crime against Yahweh. David had vigorously enforced this principle even when his enemy was King Saul.

Bathsheba sighed. "You won't harm your son, will you? Not just because he is a member of the royal family whom you have always protected, but also because of your personal love for him. So why not bring him back?"

"If I do, he'll just cause trouble for me here in Jerusalem. Of course, if I don't, he'll cause trouble anyway. I hear he's already recruiting an army of followers in Geshur."

"Do you think he'll attack Jerusalem?"

David shrugged. "Only if he's strong enough. And he isn't — yet."

"If you brought him back, you'd at least

be able to keep an eye on him."

David nodded. "I've thought of that. But I still don't want to imply approval of murder."

"Then why not bring him to Jerusalem but deny him the privileges of the palace? Keep him under house arrest at his home."

David continued to stroke his chin. "Yes, I suppose I could do that. But I still wouldn't be able to see and talk with him, like we used to. He'd be as distant as if in Geshur."

But after considerable persuasion from Joab and his other counselors, David decided to ask Absalom to return. Joab himself went to Geshur to bring him home.

Absalom's arrival in Jerusalem surprised everyone. He entered the city from the northeast, across the Kidron Brook, by the Gihon Spring, and through the Water Gate. It was like the return of an army after a successful military campaign.

Fifty armed youths led the procession, trotting in formation with their swords drawn. Then came Absalom, driving his magnificent chariot drawn by four energetic steeds of matching black colors, with silver plumes on their heads. Behind him rode his following, their mules stepping briskly to keep up with the pace. But the most awesome sight in the procession was Absalom himself.

Bathsheba watched from the palace roof as he made his way down the street toward his home. She caught her breath as her eyes were drawn toward that shining example of manhood.

He was tall, taller than his father. His shoulders were broad and his red cape flowed behind him. The breastplate gleamed in the sun. The helmet, though decorative and of little use in battle, rose tall and shining above his head, its red plume fluttering in the breeze.

And his hair! His beard was cropped short, but the hair had been allowed to grow. Long, brown, and wavy, it streamed out behind his helmet and gleamed in the sun.

He waved to people in the street, smiling, calling greetings to old acquaintances. He was saluted with cheers and shouts of welcome.

A thought popped into Bathsheba's mind as she watched. Many years ago, so she had heard, the young David had made similar displays on his return from battle. The song on the lips of the people who greeted him was, "Saul has slain his thousands, but David his tens of thousands." That had fed King Saul's jealousy and sparked the rebellion which eventually led to David's ascension to the throne. Would it be the same with Absalom?

David kept his promise of refusing to allow Absalom to come into his presence. The popular prince stayed at his house but almost every day paraded through Jerusalem in his chariot and was greeted by cheers.

Hephzibah, like everyone else in Jerusalem, had fallen madly in love with Absalom. "Ooooh, he's so wonderful!" she cooed. "So beautiful! So handsome when he smiles! And his hair! How I'd love to run my fingers through his curls!"

Were all the servants in the palace as giddy and childish as Hephzibah? Even Solomon laughed at her. At age twelve, he showed a maturity beyond the much older Hephzibah.

"Aren't you afraid your fingers will get lost in his hair?" he asked her, his eyes dancing. "Or stuck there, and you'll have to keep them there the rest of your life."

"Mmmmm," she replied, rolling her eyes. "Yes. That's where I'd keep them . . . always . . . always!"

Bathsheba laughed, but Solomon continued teasing her. "You'd have to carry his hair around, then. I've heard it's pretty heavy."

"It is." Hephzibah nodded vigorously. "He only cuts it once a year, and when he does, the hair which is cut weighs more than three pounds!"

Young Solomon whooped with laughter, and Bathsheba joined him, much to Hephzibah's disgust.

"Aw, you're just jealous, that's all." She flounced off.

Her infatuation with the comely prince reflected the viewpoint of many in Jerusalem. Others, like Bathsheba and Solomon, kept their objectivity when speaking of Absalom.

Almost every day, Absalom went to the Water Gate, where he had made his grand entrance. He would station himself just outside the gate, near the Gihon Spring where many people came to fill their water jugs. Soon he became known as an unofficial judge of Israel.

According to the rumors which reached Bathsheba's ears at the palace, Absalom intercepted many of the petitioners streaming in through the Water Gate to bring their disputes to David. There he would hear and try the cases meant for the ears of the king.

Young Solomon, accompanied by his half brother Daniel, often sat among the crowd of onlookers near the gate as Absalom judged the people. He made almost daily reports to his mother.

"Can't anybody see what he's doing?" Solomon demanded. "He greets the people as if he is their best friend. He hears their cases, then spreads on a little flattery. He doesn't even care about justice. He just makes his decisions based on what the more powerful Israelites want to hear."

"Why would he do that?" asked Bath-sheba. Since her son's twelfth birthday, she had treated him as an adult, respecting his maturity.

"He's up to something." Solomon's youthful face reflected his concern. "Everything he does, he tries to be popular. Almost as though he's trying to get everyone on his side." He nodded thoughtfully. "There's going to be trouble. I can see it coming."

"You're mistaken, son. After all, he's the king's oldest son. He doesn't need to incite a rebellion. He believes he'll be king some day."

"Maybe so." Solomon shook his head slowly. "But I hear he's raising an army in Israel. He has a few spies out there, recruiting, while Absalom is confined to Jerusalem. Why doesn't Father do something?"

"Have you spoken to him about it?" she asked.

"Oh, yes! But he just pats me on the head and tells me how nice it is I'm taking an interest in the affairs of the kingdom. He still thinks I'm a little boy."

David's mistake was understandable. As Bathsheba looked at her son, she saw a little boy. He did not have the rugged good looks of his father but reflected the delicate features and refined air of his mother's side of the family.

At age twelve, David had been given the responsibility of keeping sheep alone in the field. His anointing by the prophet Samuel occurred only about two years later. At age twelve, Solomon was still a student, learning from the priests about the law of Moses. Every day he observed the court and listened to David's decisions and rulings. But he was never given responsibility; he was considered too young.

And that was definitely a mistake, reflected Bathsheba. This boy was young only in age and looks. His mind was as mature and capable as many of David's advisers. In just a few years he would be able to succeed the aging Ahitophel as chief adviser to the king.

Then another thought struck Bathsheba. Could he be king himself, as the prophet Nathan had hinted?

She shuddered. Since the birth of Solomon, Bathsheba had been repulsed by the idea of her son being king. She had seen too much tragedy follow those who grasped for the throne. Her husband had known his share of problems, and Absalom's troubles were just beginning. David had many sons; did all of them want to be king?

Only Daniel was safe from the burdens of ambition. That blow to the head in battle had been a kindness. It had rendered him witless and incapable of becoming king. He would never know how fortunate he was.

And Solomon. The youngest of David's sons. So wise, so capable of ruling the kingdom. Bathsheba sighed. Maybe Yahweh had destined him to be king of Israel after all. If so, there was nothing she could do to prevent it.

10

One day Absalom sent David a request to leave Jerusalem. Bathsheba heard about it through Solomon, who had been in the court when Joab brought the petition before the king.

"Joab said Absalom just wanted to go to Hebron to fulfill a vow he had made to Yahweh. He wanted to offer a sacrifice at the place of his birth."

"What's wrong with that?" asked Bathsheba.

The boy shrugged. "I don't know. Yet. But he's up to something. I just know it."

"And David let him go?"

"Yes." Solomon's voice filled with sarcasm. "At the advice of the great and wise Ahitophel."

Solomon had never liked his great-grandfather. The boy had somehow rejected the legendary counselor and several times had disputed his decisions. But nobody listened to a fourteen-year-old youth when he disagreed with a white-haired experienced sage.

And so Bathsheba watched one morning from the rooftop of the palace as Absalom departed from the city. He went with his usual pomp, a bodyguard of fifty young men on foot leading the prince in his chariot, hair streaming behind. They exited the city through the southern gate, crossed the Hinnom Valley, and disappeared into the Judean hills.

After that, rumors flew around Jerusalem. They weren't idle rumors, however. David's spy network had long ago been established throughout Israel, and reports came in daily. The rebellion was under way.

During the years he had lived in Jerusalem estranged from his father, Absalom had been busy. His agents had gone out into Israel gathering supporters, recruiting troops. Now he had an army and was marching toward Jerusalem.

David called a meeting of his counselors to discuss their predicament. Solomon was there, and through him Bathsheba learned what had happened.

Many were not surprised at Absalom's rebellion. Like Solomon, they had seen it coming. David's spies had made clear that the wily prince had not been posturing while waiting in Jerusalem but had been actively fomenting the rebellion.

"We must flee," said David.

His faithful followers disagreed. They wanted to fight. Jerusalem was a stronghold. Seasoned by many battles, David's army was far superior to Absalom's raw recruits. But David held firm to his decision to leave the city and go into exile, and Solomon agreed. Avoid bloodshed now, he reasoned, and perhaps negotiate a compromise later.

Ahitophel, the wise old counselor, had defected. Shortly after Absalom left the city, he requested a leave of absence to go to his home in Giloh. He had never returned. Word came to Jerusalem that he was now Absalom's chief adviser.

Surprisingly, they exited Jerusalem without confusion. The plan was to leave by the Water Gate, cross the Brook Kidron, and climb the Mount of Olives on their way to the east. David stood by the Gihon Spring to review his followers as they left the city. Bathsheba and Solomon stood near and watched with him.

The entire palace household went with him into exile, with the exception of ten concubines who were left behind to tend the palace. These ten were carefully chosen. They were the daughters of some of the more powerful clan leaders of Israel. Their fathers had chosen to follow Absalom in the revolt, and David knew they would come to no harm when Absalom marched into the city.

Most of David's closest friends and advisers, plus their families, accompanied the king into exile. All of David's soldiers remained loyal.

David had ruled in Jerusalem for almost twenty years, and a new generation of warriors had risen around him. Gone were several of the Mighty Three and the Mighty Thirty, although many veterans remained from those elite contingents. A good many mercenaries had enlisted in the king's service, and David greeted them as they passed.

"Ittai, my friend," David shouted as a body of six hundred Gittite mercenaries approached. "Why are you here?"

The youthful face of the bearded Philistine grinned at him. "I go to fight with my sovereign," he replied.

"You don't need to. You can go back to the city. It seems only yesterday you joined my ranks. You can offer your services to the new king. He'll be glad to have you."

"No, my lord king. You are my sovereign, not Absalom. I swear by Yahweh that I will follow you to the death!"

The name of Yahweh on the young man's lips was not blasphemy. He had accepted the faith of the Israelites.

Ittai and his young Gittites were not the only ones who followed David into exile. Rank after rank marched by, saluting their king as they passed. Their families came with them, showing the completeness of their dedication.

The line was long. Many women and children accompanied the procession. David's frown deepened as he watched. Bathsheba's heart went out to him; how would he ever take care of such a multitude? Feeding them each day would be a massive undertaking. For safety, they would have to cross the Jordan River and find a place in the mountains. And no city in Trans-Jordan would be able to keep them for any length of time. Like his ancestor Moses, David would just have to learn to survive in the wilderness.

A small group of people had gathered around David as he reviewed the exiles from the city. Bathsheba looked around, noting the priests and several prophets, including her friend Nathan. David's wives and children had been among the first.

Only Bathsheba and Solomon remained at the Gihon Springs with David. The king's chronicler was there, making notes. Perhaps some day these details would be recorded officially in the Chronicles of the King — if they survived. But of course they would survive. That was why the chronicler was recording these events. He at least had faith that Yahweh was still in charge and would someday vindicate David.

The two priests, Abiathar and Zadok, stood near. They had brought the sacred ark of the covenant. Everyone assumed that wherever David went, the ark would go. This would speak eloquently to the people. They would be encouraged by this visible sign of the presence of Yahweh, always there, leading his people to whatever fate awaited them. And if it came to battle, the ark would, as ever, lead the way.

After the long procession had passed and was making its way up the Mount of Olives, David turned to his priests. "Zadok. Abiathar. You have been faithful friends for many years. You have never failed me. I am grateful. Now I am going to ask one more favor from you."

"Ask, my king," replied Zadok. He bowed his head in obeisance, gray beard reaching almost to his waist.

"We will always obey," said Abiathar.

David paused before replying, thumb and forefinger stroking his chin. "Return to Jerusalem. Take with you just enough priests to carry the sacred ark. And go with your families. Especially your sons, Ahimaaz and Jonathan."

The two priests stared at him. For a moment they could not speak. The king's order was a surprise.

"Here is my plan," David said. "I will camp at the fords of the Jordan River, at least for now. There I will await word from you as to what is happening in Jerusalem. I need to know, before I disappear into the wilderness."

The two priests absorbed David's words in silence. Bathsheba could see understanding dawn on their faces. They were going to be David's spies in Jerusalem. And their young sons would be their messengers.

They bowed their heads in acknowledgment of orders. Then the shophar sounded. The priests picked up the sacred ark and entered the Water Gate.

Their departure seemed to leave a void in the remaining exiles. Bathsheba wondered if Yahweh went with them. Would

David be blessed by God's favor in the future, or would God remain in Jerusalem with Absalom? Was the ark merely a symbol of Yahweh's presence, or was it where he lived? She shrugged. Leave that to the theologians to debate.

David next turned to the path leading east, up the Mount of Olives. The climb was a steep one, and David chose to walk it barefoot. Bathsheba understood why. The wise king showed his people his sorrow. He had led them to this suffering. And he felt deeply his guilt and shame.

A good political move, but an unwise one physically. His feet, softened by years of velvet slippers and plush carpets, brought from him winces and gasps as they pressed down on sharp stones. Soon blood appeared in his footsteps, but he pressed on.

As he approached the top, he slowed, showing signs of fatigue. He breathed heavily. Several people offered to help, but he waved them away. He set his face grimly and plodded on.

He accepted help only when young Solomon came to walk beside him. David's hand went to the youth's shoulder. It seemed to steady him, giving him leverage for each step. Bathsheba frowned. Was there a symbolism here obvious to everyone?

With Solomon's help, he finally reached the top. David — and everyone else, it seemed — breathed a sigh of relief. Solomon led him to a pile of stones, the remains of an old altar, and David sat, breathing heavily.

Nobody spoke. The sighing of the wind on the hilltop made the only sound. Those who looked behind saw a silent city awaiting its new sovereign. Those who looked ahead saw a long line of refugees heading toward the Jordan River and the wilderness.

This sad frozen moment seemed to stretch out. David sat slumped on a stone, weeping silently. Solomon stood beside him, hand on his father's shoulder. To Bathsheba it seemed everyone was waiting. Waiting for what?

The scene was interrupted by a man who pushed his way through the crowd surrounding David. An old man. A man in sorrow, for his clothes were torn and his head covered with dirt.

Bathsheba had seen him before. In David's court. Then memory came back. This was Hushai, of the Archite clan of the tribe of Benjamin. From time to time he had been one of David's counselors.

Hushai, like Ahitophel, was one of the wisest men in the kingdom. He and David, it was said, had known each other for years, going back to the time they were young men in the service of King Saul. David had become a warrior and Hushai one of the king's advisers. Although Saul too often rejected his wise counsel, Hushai remained loyal to his sovereign as long as Saul lived.

When David became king of Israel, he welcomed Hushai to his service and pleaded with him as an adviser. Reluctantly Hushai agreed, and David called on him often for advice. Now he had come to David once again, with an offer of help.

"Let me go with you, my sovereign," he pleaded. "I will serve you always."

David wearily lifted his head and stared at the old man before him. He smiled but shook his head. "No, my friend. If you go with me, you will only be a burden to me."

"But you are my king. I will follow you until I die."

Again David shook his head. "You can serve me best by going to Jerusalem and offering your services to Absalom. Say to him, 'I will advise you as I did your father.' "

"He will not accept me, my lord. He has Ahitophel."

"He *will* accept you. For I had just offered a prayer to Yahweh, asking that Ahitophel's counsel be frustrated. Then you came. I think you are the answer to this prayer."

Hushai's face slowly broke into a sly grin. "You are wise, my king. And Yahweh is truly with you. I'll do as you say."

David lowered his voice. "You can be my eyes and ears in the new king's court. When you learn Absalom's plans, tell the priests, Zadok and Abiathar, who can be trusted. Their sons, Ahimaaz and Jonathan, know how to get a message to me."

Hushai straightened his body. His chin lifted, and he seemed to shed his years. "It shall be done, my king. Yahweh go with you."

"And with you, my friend."

The crowd around David parted as Hushai marched down the hill toward Jerusalem. Abigail wondered if he were going to his death. How could even the wise Hushai be any match for her wily grandfather? Then she smiled. Ahitophel has met his match, for now he was pitted not only against Hushai — but also Yahweh. The future suddenly looked a little brighter.

11

David would not stay long on the hilltop of the Mount of Olives.

"If Absalom has any sense," he muttered, "he'll follow us immediately and attack before we can get organized. We must cross the Jordan as soon as possible."

He sent word ahead to the leaders of the column to take the northern route — the high road, through the wilderness — to the fords of the Jordan. Travel on this rugged path would be difficult but shorter, and time was important.

Someone had found a donkey for David to ride. He sat on his mount as proudly as he could, but everyone could see his exhaustion. *He's old,* thought Bathsheba. *Much too old for this kind of campaigning.*

Yet David was only a few years older than Bathsheba, and she did not feel the fatigue nearly as much. She glanced at David's men, many the same age as David. Joab and his brother Abishai, for example. They were lean and muscular, and as they pressed forward into the mountains seemed to grow stronger with each step. But then, they had spent the past twenty years in the field, fighting battles, marching all over Israel. David, meanwhile, had been confined to Jerusalem, sleeping in a bed every night, eating rich food.

But it was more than that. David had been burdened by the affairs of state and the sorrows in his family. That would age a person rapidly, Bathsheba decided.

As they neared the village of Bahurim, a man appeared on a nearby hillside. His booming voice reached out to the plodding procession.

"Get out of here, you murderer! You dog! You killed the true king Saul, and now Yahweh is paying you back! See, your own son has your kingdom now, and you have nothing! Nothing! That's because the blood of King Saul is on your hands, you murderer!"

He picked up a stone and hurled it at David. It was a long throw, but fortunately Joab and Abishai were marching close to David. Abishai raised his shield and deflected the stone before it reached his king.

"Who is that?" asked David.

Joab squinted across the valley to the

ridge where their tormentor kept pace with them. "I think that's Shimei ben Gera, a Benjaminite who was in Saul's army many years ago."

Joab's brother Abishai grunted. "This dog is as good as dead. Let me go over there and cut off his head!"

"No." David shook his head and tapped his donkey with his crop. "It is Yahweh's will. He has sent this Benjaminite to curse me. I will endure his curses, and maybe Yahweh will see my afflictions and have mercy."

Joab and Abishai shook their heads in bewilderment. They could never understand their enigmatic king. But Bathsheba thought she did. He was burdened with guilt. It began when he had summoned her to his palace that night many years ago.

That night had burned its bittersweet memory into Bathsheba's mind. That was the beginning of her new life, a life of love shared with David. But because it was born in sin, their life together had been plagued by suffering.

She no longer shared his guilt. Nathan's words had wiped it away. David evidently had never experienced the joy of forgiveness. In her mind, Yahweh was no longer a cruel punishing God, but a forgiving

Father. Nathan, who had taught her that, had apparently planted in David's mind the picture of God as chastiser burdening him and his kingdom with troubles as just payment for his sin.

The same God. Seen by one with guilt, by the other with love. Strange, reflected Bathsheba. She thought God always spoke the same message through the prophets Now it seemed God's message to each was different, suited to the individual. Another theological mystery.

They passed through Bahurim and soon the Jordan River appeared before them, twisting down a tropical valley between mountain ridges. At the foot of the mountain pass through which their rugged path had just come, they saw the military outpost and granary David himself had established a few years before on one of his campaigns to consolidate his kingdom. They could see even the crumbled remains of the ancient city of Jericho, which Joshua had leveled more than two hundred years before.

They encamped by the Jericho springs that night. They were a large company of refugees — warriors, women, children — far more than there should have been, reflected Bathsheba, for what lay ahead.

How would they be fed? The military granary here, established to supply the garrisons strategically placed at various fords of the Jordan River, would supply them for a while, but only for a few days. Then what?

Bathsheba shrugged. Yahweh would provide. She smiled to herself. That was exactly what David would say. Now she was saying it. Only a few years before she had belittled such pious trust in an invisible God to supply needs. How she had changed! Was it maturity, seeing things now with the wisdom of age and experience? Or was the God who was so real to David and Nathan now real to her also? How had this faith come to her? She shook her head. Again she decided to leave such profound matters to the theologians; she would merely live each day by faith.

In the morning David called a meeting of his close friends and advisers to plan what they should do next. Bathsheba was not present; it was men's business. Later she learned from Solomon what happened.

Everyone agreed they were in immediate danger. At any time the army of Absalom could force their fight. Joab and Abishai wanted to stay and make their stand, but David said no. He was not ready to commit the people to bloodshed in a civil war.

"Let us see what Yahweh will do," he said. "We will fight when we have to, but if we wait, we may not have to."

The warriors among them had shaken their heads and muttered, but Solomon approved his father's wisdom. "War should always be a last resort," he told his mother. "The person who wants to fight first is not smart enough to find another way."

Solomon would make a wise king, thought Bathsheba, then was appalled by the thought. The last thing she wanted was for her son to be king. Too many brothers stood ahead of him. For Solomon to be king, he would have to eliminate them, and that meant bloodshed. Yahweh would not look favorably on a king who rose to the throne over the broken bodies of his brothers.

Late that afternoon Ahimaaz and Jonathan, sons of the priests Zadok and Abiathar, arrived. They were in their late teens, short beards barely covering their faces. They bubbled with excitement at their recent adventures.

Immediately David called a conference of his advisers. With the rest, Bathsheba trembled with anticipation. Everyone knew these young men brought news of events in Jerusalem which would determine their future.

The conference did not last long. When it broke up, just before sunset, the news flew around the camp: *We're moving. Now!*

The camp buzzed with speculation as they hastily packed for the journey. Fortunately the Jordan was at its dry season low stage, and they forded the swift current easily. Word quickly spread: "We're going to Mahanaim!"

Solomon, who had attended the conference, relayed to Bathsheba what had happened. "Ahimaaz and Jonathan had quite a time getting the news to us," he reported. "They had a narrow escape at Bahurim."

"Tell me first about Absalom," said Bathsheba as she trudged through the darkness with a heavy pack on her back. "Is his army close?"

"Nobody knows for sure." Solomon's pace was brisk, reflecting his youth and excitement. "Absalom hadn't made his decision before the boys left Jerusalem. Their fathers thought the news couldn't wait."

"What happened?"

"As I understand it," Solomon answered, adjusting his pack in midstride, "Absalom couldn't make up his mind. Ahitophel wanted to strike immediately. Send the army out now, and catch us before we're organized. Smart advice." Solomon grinned. "Everybody knows Grandfather Ahitophel is the smartest man in the kingdom."

"But if he had followed Grandfather's counsel, wouldn't they be here by now? Even if they had taken the lower road to Jericho, they should have attacked us today."

Solomon nodded. "That's why I think Absalom didn't take his advice. They aren't here yet, but Father couldn't take the chance. They might come tomorrow."

Yes, reflected Bathsheba, caution was the best policy. Aloud she said, "But why wouldn't Absalom take Grandfather's advice? It doesn't make sense."

Again Solomon grinned in his boyish way. "Hushai. He gave advice to Absalom opposed to Ahitophel's."

"What did he say?"

"That it would be foolish to strike now. He told about Father's experienced army, seasoned by many battles, compared to Absalom's raw recruits. It would be better to sound the trumpet again in Israel. In a few months he would have superiority in numbers to counterbalance Father's veterans."

Bathsheba nodded. "And by that time, we'll be ready for them."

"Exactly. And you can be sure Father will choose his own time and place to meet them."

So. David's placing of Hushai in the court of Absalom had been shrewd. Although why Absalom would follow the counsel of Hushai over Ahitophel was a mystery. Unless Yahweh's hand was guiding David's affairs.

She glanced over her shoulder apprehensively, as though looking for a column of Absalom's troops following them. All she could see was darkness. They had already entered the mountains and soon would be on the ancient King's Highway which led to Mahanaim.

Solomon noticed her backward glance and laughed. "Don't worry, Mother. Father thought about that, too. He left Ittai the Gittite back there at the ford."

Ittai. Bathsheba recalled the young Philistine with his six hundred mercenaries who had insisted on staying with David. Mercenaries! Hired soldiers. Yes, they would be given the dirty job of staying behind to delay the enemy should he follow. That was the lot of men who made war their profession. Whether they survived or died making a last stand depended on whether Absalom followed Ahitophel's or Hushai's advice.

On through the night they trudged, and the next day too. Everyone was exhausted. Bathsheba could do no more than concentrate on placing one foot ahead of the other. Every bone in her body ached with fatigue.

Partway through the day, Ahimaaz and Jonathan joined them. Their youthful vigor lent a momentary lift to the weary travelers. The young men went from one group to another, bursting with enthusiasm, telling the story of their narrow escape from Jerusalem.

"We were staying at En Rogel while we waited for the message we would take to the king," said Ahimaaz.

En Rogel was a well in the Kidron Valley, just south of Jerusalem. Their parents had stationed them there so no one would notice them in Jerusalem. Already suspected, the priests were watched constantly by Absalom's spies.

Jonathan continued the story. "We got word through a servant girl that Hushai wanted us to run to King David, with the message that he must cross the Jordan River as soon as possible."

Ahimaaz continued, "That girl's boyfriend did us in. He told Absalom's spies, and they came after us. We barely got away."

"Where did you go?" asked Bathsheba.

"We took the mountain road, same as you did," replied Jonathan. "When we got to Bahurim, we knew they were right behind us. We had to find a place to hide."

Ahimaaz interrupted. "We hid in a well. Some shepherd and his wife let us down it, then covered it with a lid and scattered grain on the top."

"Who were these two people who hid you?" asked Bathsheba. David would want to reward them later.

Jonathan shrugged. "I don't know. We didn't have time to ask their names."

"Did Absalom's men look for you?" asked Bathsheba.

"They sure did! It seemed like a long time in that well," replied Ahimaaz.

"And it was dark and cold down there," added Jonathan.

"Weren't you scared?" Bathsheba had forgotten her weariness as she listened to their story.

"No." Ahimaaz waved his hand. "Not

us. We're warriors!"

Bathsheba stifled a smile. These boys were still boys. They didn't have enough maturity to admit being afraid. If she had asked the same question of Joab and Abishai, veteran warriors, they probably would have admitted fear without hesitation.

The exhausted company arrived at Mahanaim in the late afternoon. There they were met cordially by the city fathers and quartered in the houses of people all over the city. Bathsheba and Solomon were assigned to the home of a man and his wife, who greeted them warmly, fed them, and led them to the rooftop, where pallets for sleeping awaited them. In a few minutes they were asleep, and slumbered heavily through the night and on into the next day.

Bathsheba woke in the morning with the sun on her face and the noises of the city in the air. Solomon's bed was empty. That young man had obviously not needed as much sleep as she and was no doubt down below speaking with their host and learning the latest news.

She looked out over the parapet of the rooftop at the city. The name Mahanaim, meaning "double camp," fit the broad valley. Here their ancestor Jacob had divided his large family and possessions into two camps. If his angry brother Esau found them, he would only be able to destroy half. Here also Ishbosheth, after the death of his father King Saul, had established his capital in a pitiful attempt to rule what was left of his father's kingdom. In one of these houses he had been assassinated, opening the throne of Israel to David.

Though not as large as Jerusalem, the city was as easily defensible. The strong wall which surrounded the residential area could hold an army at bay for a long time. No wonder David had chosen this city as his place of refuge. Absalom, if he attacked here, would have a long siege to dislodge the forces of David. Bathsheba shuddered at the thought of Mahanaim under attack, at the weeks — or months — of siege and suffering. She hoped it would never come to that.

Nevertheless, this would be her home for a while. For how long? Probably months. The city was not especially wealthy, despite its favorable location for trade on the well-traveled King's Highway. How could several hundred refugees find enough to keep them alive here? Through the generosity of their hosts? That was asking a lot of these people.

"Well, Yahweh," she whispered. "Here we are again. In your hands. Take care of us, please."

Her prayer brought relief. She turned to go down to the courtyard to join her son in becoming better acquainted with her host and hostess.

12

Yahweh had indeed blessed the refugees, for offers of help came from all over Israel. Many of the people in David's kingdom remained loyal to the king, and sent him gifts of food and soldiers. In the weeks that followed, they came from Dan to Beersheba, bringing herds and grain and the many small items of housewares the refugees had left behind on their hurried departure from Jerusalem. Young men, eager to profit from the spoils of war, joined David in the hope that if he won, they would gain power and influence in the kingdom.

The loyalty of so many was encouraging to Bathsheba. David's son Absalom had all the magnetism of his father, and he too attracted followers. But David, while older, still held the admiration and love of large numbers of Israelites.

Something else came to David during those weeks he was a refugee in Mahanaim — intelligence reports. David had spies everywhere, not only in Jerusalem but all over Israel. Every day the reports arrived, and all the people of David's entourage knew everything that was happening almost as soon as it took place.

Bathsheba heard, for example, that her grandfather Ahitophel was dead — by his own hand. When Absalom had taken Hushai's advice and rejected Ahitophel's, the shrewd old counselor read the future. Their best chance of destroying David had evaporated when they didn't follow and strike when the fleeing refugees were disorganized. Now, with David's veterans ready to make their stand, Ahitophel saw little hope for success, though Absalom's army had numerical superiority. Knowing the fate which awaited him when David returned to power, he had gone home and hanged himself.

Bathsheba did not mourn him. He had never been close to her, and when she married David, he had, like most of the people of Jerusalem, turned his back on her. Then at the end he had turned traitor. Now, thankfully, he would no longer be advising Absalom.

David's spies reported that Absalom's army was finally on the march. They came in large numbers, having sounded the trumpet in Israel and conscripted many soldiers. Their plan was to attack from the north, coming through the Forest of Ephraim to confront David and his forces in the broad valley of Mahanaim.

David called a meeting of his counselors to plan for battle. Solomon attended this council of war.

"Father divided our army into three divisions," he told his mother. "As you might expect, Joab will lead one and Abishai the other. But you'll never guess who will command the third!"

"No I can't, son," Bathsheba replied. "You know I'm no good at military matters. Tell me."

"Ittai the Gittite. With all the veteran warriors around him, men from his Mighty Thirty, Father bypassed them and chose a foreign mercenary. Can you believe that?"

Bathsheba smiled, as always amazed that her young son could grasp the affairs of state and military strategies so easily.

"Maybe it was a reward for staying with us, when he could have gone back," she replied.

"No, it was more than that. I think he sees leadership qualities in that Gittite. Father always was good at picking his men. Or maybe he just wanted a new young face to lead his troops, rather than the same old people who have been leading all these years."

"Weren't some of the veterans jealous?"

"I don't think so." Solomon rubbed his chin with his thumb and forefinger, as his father often did. "In fact, I think they welcomed the change and offered their congratulations and encouragement to Ittai. I think they consider him their own protégé and want to help him."

"You're not going out to battle, are you son?"

"No, Mother. They think I'm too young. It's just as well. I wouldn't be much good to them anyway."

The boy did not seem in the least disappointed. How unlike other boys his age! Every young man wanted to be a warrior, thinking this was the epitome of maturity and manhood. But not Solomon. He was more interested in strategy and statehood than warfare. In fact, his favorite saying was, "Fighting is for those not smart enough to find another way."

Their friend Daniel would be going to battle, however. The son of Queen Abigail might not be mentally equipped to rule the kingdom, but he was physically equipped to fight. His muscular body and fighting skills were unimpaired by the blow to the head. He had been assigned to the division commanded by Abishai.

Jonathan and Ahimaaz, the young sons of the priests, were eager to go. To them it would be another adventure, much like the one in which they escaped from Jerusalem and brought the message to the king. To their delight, they were assigned to Joab's division.

Solomon's next statement surprised Bathsheba. "Even the king wanted to go!"

Bathsheba shook her head slowly. Her husband should know better. He was not physically up to the rigors of a hard campaign. But maybe the excitement of this grand adventure had stirred memories of other years and campaigns.

"Will he go?" she asked, voice trembling.

Solomon laughed. "Don't worry, Mother. Everybody protested so loudly he gave in and agreed to stay in Mahanaim. Joab put it best. He said, 'If we lose this battle, the enemy won't care whether any of us live or die. But they'll be looking for you. You are worth more than ten thousand of us, and we want you alive!' "

Bathsheba nodded. David would bow before this impeccable logic. His place was here, commanding the broader picture, rather than on the battlefield with its limited vision.

"Father himself picked the part of the country where our forces will meet them: the Forest of Ephraim, before they arrive in the Mahanaim Valley. They have chariots, and they'll be useless there. I don't know why anybody trusts in chariots anyway; they're of no strategic value unless you're on a broad plain, and there aren't many plains in this part of the country. No army of foot soldiers with any sense would meet charioteers in battle on open ground."

Bathsheba had little interest in the plan of battle Solomon described to her. Ittai's division would meet the enemy head on, and Joab and Abishai would attack the flanks. In the forest it would be one-on-one, and David's veterans would have the advantage. Solomon obviously approved of his father's strategy, and he prattled on with great enthusiasm.

Only one part of the plan sparked interest for Bathsheba.

"Father told them not to harm Absalom," said Solomon. "I gather he still loves his son, although after all this, I don't see why. The best thing that could happen would be for him to die in battle. If he lives, what will Father do with him? He can't just let him go; Absalom would only start another rebellion and we'd have to go through all this again. But keeping him a prisoner wouldn't be good either, because he's the king's son. Not only that, he's the oldest son, except Daniel. Would he succeed Father some day? After all he's done? Better he die in battle."

Bathsheba nodded. "Don't forget the king's rule: never harm Yahweh's Anointed, or his sons. He established that a long time ago, in the days of Saul and Jonathan."

Solomon grinned. "It's a good rule. Protects all of us. But don't forget, Absalom himself violated that rule when he killed Amnon. The punishment for disobeying it is death. Now there's a real dilemma. If the king's son takes the life of a king's son, who will execute the king's son? Nobody will dare."

"So the problem remains," mused Bathsheba. "If Absalom is captured, what will become of him?"

"That's a riddle worthy of the best wit in Israel. What's the answer?"

"It's in Yahweh's hands," replied Bathsheba.

Solomon laughed bitingly. "Yes, I suppose so. Maybe he's the only one smart enough to solve the riddle."

Bathsheba glanced sharply at her son. Was he being sarcastic? It sounded like something she would have said only a few years ago. It bordered on blasphemy.

How did her perceptive son feel about God? He never talked much about Yahweh. Did he believe? Surely he must. Anyone with this much intelligence could see the hand of the deity in all the affairs of Israel, and especially the providential care which followed the life and career of David ben Jesse. Even now, so far from Jerusalem and the ark of the covenant, Yahweh's loving hand ruled the affairs of Israel. It was so plain to her. Why would it not be equally clear to Solomon?

The next morning the army marched out to battle the invaders in the Forest of Ephraim to the north. They paraded in review past the king and Solomon as they stood at the north gate of Mahanaim.

Bathsheba watched from the rooftop of her host's house, along with all the other inhabitants of Mahanaim. Were these men going to their deaths? Would the next army she saw on the road from the north be the followers of David returning with news of victory? Or would it be the enemy, coming

139

to execute the king and destroy their lives?

Only Yahweh knew the answer to that question. Yahweh, solver of riddles. The one whose invisible presence stood beside the aging king and his clever son as they stood by the gate of the city to bid farewell to the departing troops.

Yahweh, please! Give us victory!

13

Now that the army had gone, there was little for David to do. He spent more time with Bathsheba and Solomon, often watching and waiting at the city gate.

As in most fortified cities, the two-story gatehouse consisted of a large room on the first floor with two heavy gates, an inner and an outer. Over it was a second room. Watchmen were stationed on the roof above. David often watched from the roof, but sometimes he paced the floor of the gatehouse below. Bathsheba and Solomon often joined him in this room.

"When will we hear?" he asked for the seventy-seventh time, or so it seemed to Bathsheba. "Five days! Five days and not a word. Not even a message from Joab saying the troops are in place and awaiting the ambush in the Forest of Ephraim."

"You're wearing a groove in the floor of the gatehouse, Father." Solomon sat on a bench, smiling wryly. "If you walk from the other two corners for a change, you'll form an X. Then, if you just weave a few circles, you'll create a design worthy of —"

"It is *not* funny!" David paused in his pacing to glare at his son. "Our whole future depends on what happens just a few miles north of us. When you're older, you'll take these things more seriously."

"I've heard that when you were a young man, you laughed loudest when the danger was greatest. Is this what maturity does to a person?"

David shook his head but did not reply. He was clearly in no mood to exchange witticisms with his clever son. He did, however, quit his now self-conscious pacing and sit on the bench beside Solomon. Bathsheba could see him squirming, however, and wondered how long it would be before he resumed pacing.

Inside the walls, Mahanaim bustled with its daily routine. Now that most of the men had gone, the people reverted to their usual quiet life, if life in a city could be called quiet. Bathsheba heard the chatter of women as they passed on the street, and the excited calls of children playing. A pleasant, peaceful city. Were they aware of what was happening nearby?

"My lord king!" The excited voice of the watchman came down to them from above.

"Someone is coming! A runner."

"Is he alone?" asked David.

"Yes, sir."

"Ah, at last. A messenger. Now we'll know something."

"Wait, my lord king!" shouted the watchman. "I see another one. The second one . . . I think . . . is black. Yes, I see him now. He is one of the mercenaries from Cush."

"Who will arrive first?" asked David.

"The young man. I think . . . yes! He's Ahimaaz the son of Zadok the priest!"

David's face broke into a grin. "Fine! He does well as a bearer of news."

The gate was open, and David walked out on the road to meet the youth. Solomon, Bathsheba, and several others followed.

Ahimaaz stumbled in his weariness as he approached. He gasped for breath, holding his side. "It's . . . all right!" he panted. "Yahweh . . . has given us victory! He . . . he has destroyed . . . the rebels who — who dared to rise up against you!"

The boy's last few steps were agony for him. Bathsheba noted the red face, twisted now behind the stubble of his youthful beard. He sank to his knees before the king, gulping down great drafts of air.

David loomed over him. "And Absalom? What of my son? Is he all right?"

The youth looked up. It seemed to Bathsheba his face took on a new agony.

"I don't know, my lord king. Everything was so confused . . . and everyone was shouting. . . . I didn't hear. I just don't know. . . ."

He knows, thought Bathsheba. *He's afraid to tell.*

David nodded, his face serious. "We'll wait," he said brusquely.

Ahimaaz slumped to the ground, panting. Bathsheba sensed that the youth was relieved he didn't have to answer the king's question.

The second messenger came toward them, loping with long deliberate strides. He was tall, muscular, and completely without hair. His black skin glistened with sweat. Because he had not sprinted, he was not exhausted and out of breath.

A Cushite, mused Bathsheba. One of the mercenaries from Upper Egypt. There were several from that African clan in David's army. Good loyal soldiers, whom David welcomed and trusted.

"My lord king!" His thick lips fumbled with the words in an unfamiliar language. "Good news! Today Yahweh saved you from those who rebelled against you."

"And Absalom?" demanded the king. "What about my son? Is he all right?"

The big Cushite grinned. "May all the rebels against my king be like that young man!"

David gasped. It seemed to Bathsheba that everyone else in that small group gathered around them gasped also. They all knew what those words meant to the king. All except the Cushite.

"No!" David shouted the words. "No! No! No!" He sank to his knees, and his hands went to his face. "No! It can't be true! Absalom! Oh, my son! Oh, if only I could have died in your place! No!"

He tore his robe and scooped up a handful of dust, which he threw on his head. He put his face on the ground, forehead in the dust.

The people around him backed away — all except Bathsheba and Solomon. They went to the king.

"Upstairs!" hissed Bathsheba. "The people must not see him like this. Not now!"

Solomon nodded. He grasped immediately the political significance of the king appearing sorrowful at this good news. Together mother and son lifted David to his feet and steered him toward the steps leading to the room above the gatehouse. He allowed them to lead him without protest, all the while moaning.

David fell on the floor of the upstairs guard room and would not be comforted.

"We'd best leave him alone," said Bathsheba. "He needs time."

Solomon nodded and spoke to a watchman. "Stay out of this room, and don't allow anyone in. The king needs time to grieve for his son."

The watchman, an older man, nodded respectfully to the boy. "Yes, my prince," he replied.

Bathsheba and Solomon went below.

"Let's talk to Ahimaaz," said Bathsheba. "Maybe we'll find out what happened."

That young man had recovered from his exertions and stood with the others by the gate.

"Come, walk with us, Ahimaaz," invited Bathsheba. She turned to walk into the city. Solomon and Ahimaaz followed.

"Yes, Queen Bathsheba," replied Ahimaaz.

Bathsheba's heart leaped. No one had ever called her that before. No one had called anyone "Queen" since the time of Abigail. Was it just this young man . . . or were all the soldiers now saying that? She shoved the thought aside. The boy must be questioned.

"What really happened out there?" she demanded.

Ahimaaz took a deep breath. He was still panting a little.

"We were fighting in the forest," he said. "Everything was confused. Nobody could see anything. But we knew we were winning, because the enemy retreated, and all the dead bodies seemed to be those of Absalom's army."

"You were in Joab's division, weren't you?" asked Solomon.

"Yes, my prince. Then some young warrior, I don't know who, told us that Absalom was caught in a tree —"

"In a tree!" Solomon stared at the youth. "You mean by his long hair?"

Ahimaaz shrugged. "The hair held him there, but he actually hung by his head. Then Joab said to the warrior, 'What! You saw him and didn't kill him? I would have given you ten coins of silver, and even a warrior's belt if you had!' "

Bathsheba nodded. Ten coins of silver was the usual reward given to a soldier on the spot, after he had just performed some extraordinary feat in combat. The warrior's belt meant a position of authority.

Ahimaaz continued his story. "The young man told Joab, 'Even if you gave me ten thousand pieces of silver, I wouldn't have done it. I heard the king's order about killing his son, and I knew what he would do.' "

So . . . David's long-established policy against killing a son of Yahweh's Anointed was understood by everybody.

Ahimaaz continued, grinning. "You should have heard Joab. He cussed out that young soldier something fierce! Then he made him take us to Absalom. Sure enough, there he was, hanging from a tree. He was still alive, too, although helpless and in great pain."

"What did Joab do?" asked Bathsheba, although she anticipated his answer.

Ahimaaz's grin faded. "He rammed his spear into his chest. Then he drew his sword and stabbed him with that. And also his dagger. Then he stepped back and motioned for us to do the same."

Ahimaaz paused. He lowered his eyes. Finally he spoke, softly.

"We . . . obeyed."

Bathsheba shuddered. She wished she hadn't asked for the grisly details.

The youth hurried on with his story.

"Then we buried Absalom in a pit and piled stones on his grave. Joab gave orders to sound the trumpet and stop the slaughter, because the battle was over."

A pile of stones in the Forest of Ephraim. What an ignominious end to the career of this ambitious prince of Israel. Bathsheba recalled the tomb Absalom had constructed for himself in the King's Valley just outside Jerusalem. He had erected a stone monument so all would remember him.

She glanced at Solomon. Would he have the same thought she had at that moment? *This is what happens to kings' sons who reach for the throne with bloodshed.*

The soldiers from the victorious army began to filter back into Mahanaim, and the city began to celebrate. They would know of David's reaction, and undoubtedly it dampened much of their celebrations. Bathsheba felt she should try to bring David out of his sorrow. She had done it before, years ago when Abigail died. Maybe she could again.

She climbed the steps to the guardhouse. The watchman on guard at the door let her pass.

David still lay on the floor, weeping. He had torn his clothes, and his hair was covered with dust.

"You are Yahweh's Anointed," she said softly. "You have a duty to your people."

Her statement had no effect on the prostrate man before her. The words had worked when Abigail died. But not this time. She wondered what it would take to bring him out of his sorrow. Something would have to be done; the king could not afford to grieve now.

Suddenly Joab burst into the room. He still wore his armor, but his helmet had been discarded. His dirty face and uncombed hair and beard made him look like a wild man.

"We just saved your life!" he shouted at the king. "And the lives of your sons, your daughters, your wives and concubines, then you act like this. You make us feel ashamed, like we did something wrong!"

Only Joab would speak that way to the king of Israel. Only Joab. The man who had just disobeyed a direct order not to harm the king's son.

"Why is it," Joab continued, his voice harsh, "that you love those who hate you, and hate those who love you? It looks like you don't care about your own men. Why, if Absalom had lived and all of us died, you'd probably like that, wouldn't you?"

David still lay on the floor, unmoving. But he had stopped his moaning and wailing.

"Remember: you are Yahweh's Anointed. Now get up. Go out there and speak to your men. Tell them you're happy about the victory we won for you. Because if you don't, I swear by Yahweh, they'll all desert you, and you'll be worse off than ever!"

Joab turned and marched out of the room. Bathsheba remained, hardly daring to breathe. No sound came from the prostrate man on the floor.

Solomon stepped into the room behind her. He stared at his father. He had undoubtedly heard every word of Joab's outburst, as had the watchman and several others.

Then Bathsheba knew what to say. "Quick, Solomon, run to the house. Bring a clean robe for your father. I'll bring him water to bathe with. He must look nice when he speaks to his men."

She spoke loud enough for David to hear. Then she followed Solomon out of the room and found a basin. When she returned to the room, David was on his feet. He stared at her. She said nothing but placed the bowl of water on the bench and left the room, just as Solomon returned with a clean robe, a comb, and a vial of oil.

When she descended to the first floor of the gatehouse, a crowd had already assembled. Word of Joab's speech had evidently spread rapidly, and the soldiers and people of the city stood quietly, curious as to what the king would do next.

In a few moments he descended the stairs, looking refreshed. He wore the clean robe. His hair and beard were combed and oiled. His eyes were still sad but steady.

"Thank you, men," he said quietly. In the stillness, his voice carried. "Now . . . let's go home."

That was all he said, but it was enough. A cheer erupted from the crowd. Then the victory celebration began.

The next day, they left Mahanaim on their way home to Jerusalem.

14

Before leaving Mahanaim, David sent dispatches to Jerusalem. He informed the priests, Zadok and Abiathar, as well as Hushai and any other counselors who remained true to him, that he was on his way home. They were to ensure the loyalty of the people of Israel, and the elders of all the tribes were personally to invite the king — the *real* king — to come home.

He would wait for their answer, encamped on the eastern side of the Jordan River. Crossing the Jordan, then, became the symbol for all people to note. Once he crossed the river, he was king again. But the people of Israel would have to invite him.

David was especially concerned about Judah. His own tribe had been the first to defect. He had been dismayed and hurt by this rebellion by his own people and wanted to test their loyalty now.

Young Solomon was among the first fully to grasp the complicated political situation, and he explained it to Bathsheba.

"Most of the rebels were Judahites," he told her. "At least in the beginning. Absalom was tremendously popular there, and that's where the rebellion started."

"But why?" asked Bathsheba. "David was popular there, too. He was their king before he became king of all Israel."

Solomon shrugged. "Maybe they saw in Absalom what they saw in Father thirty years ago — a young, vigorous warrior, immensely attractive, who could charm the birds out of the trees."

"But what has David done to turn the people of Judah against him? Hasn't he made the kingdom secure, defeated the Philistines and all our other enemies, built safe roads, established trade with the powerful nations around us, and made us proud to be a great nation of the world?"

Solomon nodded, his thumb and forefinger stroking his smooth chin. "Yes, he has done all those things. It just shows how fickle the people are. I think they were blinded by Absalom. When the sun shone on him, it glistened so much you couldn't see anything else."

He has a way of saying things, mused Bathsheba. *For a teenager, he's so wise.* She had heard the talk among the leaders of

David's court that the boy was wise enough to be a worthy successor to the throne. She didn't like that talk, but she had to admit it was true. Her son would make a good king. Much better than any of his older brothers.

His older brothers! This brought her a thought she hadn't considered before. Now that Absalom was dead, who would be next in line for the throne?

Adonijah.

He was the son of David's wife Haggith, whom David had married while king of Judah only. She was the widow of a wealthy Israelite whom Joab had raided back in the days when Judah and Israel were unofficially at war.

Adonijah had grown up in David's family as a dutiful son. He never expected to be his father's successor. There were too many brothers ahead of him, and Adonijah had never been particularly ambitious. Attractive, yes — all David's sons were good looking and charming. Only a few were ambitious, and Adonijah wasn't one. He had remained loyal to David during Absalom's revolt.

Bathsheba frowned, looking at Solomon. She couldn't help comparing the two boys. Boys? Adonijah was in his early thirties;

Solomon was not even half his age. Yet she could not deny it: Solomon would make a far better king.

She shuddered. She did not want Solomon to be king.

At one time, she herself had been ambitious and shameless in her attempts to satisfy her goals. But no longer. The death of her first-born son — and subsequent talks with the prophet Nathan — had purged her of selfish desires. She had come to a conviction that Yahweh the living God did not tolerate vain aspirations. Better to leave the outcome of events in God's hands. Such were the lessons of Absalom — and David also, for that matter.

Solomon, though young, had never expressed a desire to be king. He had seemed to agree when she talked with him about reaching for the throne over the blood of his brothers. At least he had appeared to agree. You never knew what was going on in that clever young mind.

That mind grasped the significance of David's camp on the eastern side of the Jordan River. He explained to Bathsheba how ingenious his father's plan was: to unify the tribes in their invitation to David to be king over them once more.

"They will scramble to send their representatives to the ford of the Jordan, trying to be the first, and thus gain the favor of the king." He grinned. "And they know the king will be watching."

To Bathsheba's astonishment — and Solomon's puzzlement — the first tribe to come to the Jordan was Judah. David's own tribe had been the first to follow Absalom into rebellion.

While they waited on the eastern side of the Jordan River for the invitation of the tribes, Bathsheba and Solomon learned what had prompted Judah's capitulation. At first it was just a rumor. Later, the truth came out.

David had secretly sent word to the priests in Jerusalem to go to Judah and talk with the elders. He offered amnesty to the Judahite soldiers who had followed Absalom and survived the battle of the Forest of Ephraim.

To emphasize this amnesty — or perhaps to reassure the people of Judah that he meant what he promised — he fired Joab and appointed Amasa commander-in-chief of all the army of Israel.

Amasa! He, like Joab and Abishai, was David's nephew. David had two sisters, Zeruiah, mother of Joab and Abishai, and Abigail, mother of Amasa. Strange, that

Amasa's mother bore the same name as the former queen of Israel.

Amasa had been Absalom's right-hand man. The veteran soldier had been one of the few of David's Mighty Thirty to defect and follow Absalom. He had been a popular hero in Judah and one reason so many Judahites joined the rebellion. Absalom had appointed him his general. Amasa had led the army to defeat in the battle of the Forest of Ephraim and had barely escaped with his life.

Now David offered him the highest position in the army of Israel — to supplant Joab! Thus David's amnesty to all the Judahite rebels would be guaranteed.

The offer delighted the people of Judah, and large numbers of them came to the fords of the Jordan to welcome their king.

The offer delighted Judah — but enraged Joab. When he heard about it, he cursed furiously and stormed off to his own tent, where he remained, sulking.

"He'll come around," David said. "I know Joab. No one in Israel is more loyal to me. You'll see."

Bathsheba wondered about David's ability to forgive so easily. Could he trust Amasa? He had betrayed his king once. She shook her head. Her husband was just too softhearted. He could forgive anybody — except himself.

And Joab. Had he just made a powerful enemy? Would Joab turn against him now? Had David forgiven him, too?

On the day appointed to cross the Jordan River, she had another occasion to observe David's readiness to offer amnesty. It involved Shimei ben Gera.

Bathsheba watched as that ancient warrior splashed across the shallow stream to stand before David. He went to his knees and bowed low before him.

"My lord king. Please don't hold in your mind the words I spoke to you before. They were wrong. I have sinned. Please forgive me."

Bathsheba recalled this man clearly. Just a few months ago, while David and all his people were fleeing Jerusalem, Shimei had cursed him. Just outside the village of Bahurim, on the mountain road to Jericho, he had stood on a nearby hilltop and hurled stones and insults at David. Now here he was, seeking forgiveness.

"Let me kill him," growled Abishai. "He deserves it. He cursed Yahweh's Anointed."

"No! Don't talk like that, you son of Zeruiah!"

Bathsheba gasped when she heard his words. Abishai set his jaw and turned away. What was David doing? He had just called Abishai "son of Zeruiah," reminding him he was the brother of Joab, who was in disgrace. It almost seemed David was turning his back on loyal friends and embracing his enemies.

David spoke louder than he needed to, perhaps so the Judahites on the other bank of the Jordan could hear him. "This is not a day for executions. This is a day for celebrations. No one shall die today, because I am once again king of Israel!"

He turned to the man who had prostrated himself before his king. "You shall not die. I swear before Yahweh!"

Bathsheba did not need Solomon to explain David's actions. It was more than pure kindness; it was a shrewd political move. Amnesty to his former enemies. Forgiveness for Shimei. Appointment of Amasa to commander-in-chief. Compromises with the new factions which had arisen in Israel. Soon all the people would know about David's actions, which might rebond them to their king.

Then David stepped into the shallow stream of the Jordan River and marched to the other side. He was greeted by cheers from the assembled Judahites. They waved palm branches and shouted, "Praise to Yahweh's Anointed! Blessed is he who comes in Yahweh's Name!"

From Jericho to Jerusalem — on the lower route this time, which was easier to travel — the people lined the road, waving palm branches and shouting the same words. David rode on a donkey now, proudly, waving and smiling to his people.

However, as Bathsheba noted from her place in the triumphant procession, most of the people who greeted him and cheered were Judahites. Where were the other tribes of Israel?

They approached the city from the south, and David decided to enter by the Water Gate, the same gate by which he had left. The people would not fail to see the significance of that entrance. It was as symbolic as the crossing of the Jordan.

They marched triumphantly up the Kidron Valley, past the Gihon Spring, into the Water Gate. Everywhere people greeted them with cheering and palm branches. On every lip were the words, "Yahweh's Anointed!"

David had come home. He had left as a refugee, an exile from his own house. Now he returned a king.

Yahweh's king, thought Bathsheba with satisfaction. Yahweh's Anointed. For without Yahweh, his kingdom could not be secure.

15

At the palace, Bathsheba took charge of organizing their return. She gave orders to begin once again the long and complicated process of organizing the kitchens to produce at least one major meal every day, to tend the garden in the inner courtyard, to assign rooms and spaces to everyone, including a few new palace residents they had picked up along the way.

And the people respected her. David's wives, who had once shut her out, now turned to her for leadership. They seemed to say to her, *You have earned the right to be the First Wife.*

And the servants — they called her Queen Bathsheba now. This was the second time she had been called that, the other time by young Ahimaaz a few weeks ago. She shook her head. Not since the time of Queen Abigail had anyone been called that. They thought of her not only as First Wife but now called her Queen of Israel! She smiled wryly. Less than twenty years ago, she had fantasized about being called that. Now she didn't care about power. She had been purged of ambition. Nevertheless it was gratifying to hear the name "Queen Bathsheba" on the lips of the servants.

What had changed her? Was it attaining the power she once sought and finding it hollow? Was it the creeping maturity of old age, which thickened her stomach, swelled her breasts, rounded her shoulders — and mellowed her need for power? Was it the driving search for peace in her life now, after all the struggle and challenges and turmoil she had experienced? Or was it something more profound — the touch of God's hand, which had given her a completely new perspective on what was important and what not?

She shrugged. These were the kind of questions young Solomon would enjoy discussing. But she had fewer philosophical bones in her body. She was a plodder — taking each day as it came, letting others seek to understand the bigger picture.

She tried to be kind to the ten concubines David had left behind to keep house. Like everyone else who had been in exile, she learned their story now.

Hushai told it. He spoke in the royal

court, now gathered in the Assembly Hall to resume the business of the kingdom. Bathsheba watched from the sidelines while the gray-haired counselor stood before the king and told the story.

"Then the young rebel Absalom turned to Ahitophel and said, 'What shall I do about my father's concubines?'

"And Ahitophel, whose advice everyone respected, as you well know, my king, replied, 'Lie with them. Then all Israel will know you are now the true king.' "

Bathsheba, like every person there, understood this strategy. When one king succeeds another, whether by death or conquest, he becomes husband of all the former ruler's wives and concubines. The people of Israel would not miss the significance of this symbolic act.

"So the rebel erected a tent on the roof of this very house. And he went in to each of the ten concubines, one at a time, while all Israel watched."

Bathsheba wondered how the fathers of the concubines felt about this. Perhaps they had been agreeable. They had given their daughters to one king in hopes of gaining influence. Why not to another? Whichever king showed them the most favors, that one should have their daughters. The fathers had guessed wrong in this case, however.

But what of the poor girls? They were still in their teens, with a productive life still ahead. Like all young women, they had no say in decisions which affected their lives. If the decisions were good, they prospered; if bad, they suffered. In this case, the decisions were bad. This became evident in David's next words.

"Let a house be prepared for them in the city. There they will be kept at our expense. They will not be harmed. But they will never marry."

He turned to Sheva, his young scribe, who sat cross-legged on the edge of the dais, the ever-present scroll in his lap and a quill pen in his hand.

"So let it be done, and so let it be recorded in the Chronicles of the King."

So many of David's decisions ended with these words! The Chronicles were growing, mused Bathsheba. Sheva had succeeded an older scribe who had been appointed when David first came to Jerusalem. Everything was written down. If the scrolls survived, they would contain a clear record of all the king's deeds. But only the good deeds, however.

Bathsheba frowned. What about the bad

deeds? Like the one big sin which had darkened David's otherwise illustrious life? The one which had brought her to the palace?

She had heard that this incident had found its way into the Sacred Story, which was recited in the homes of the people. Ever since the time of Moses, the people followed a quaint custom. On the Sabbath, the family would gather and the patriarch would tell the story, recited word-for-word from memory. It began with the creation of the world, the stories of Adam and Eve, and continued through Abraham, and Jacob, and Moses, and Joshua. Now the story included the saga of David, and seemed to focus on his sin with Bathsheba.

But that story was never included in the official Chronicles of the King. The written record might survive the centuries, but would the spoken record? Probably not. And yet . . . it had survived all the centuries so far.

Bathsheba shrugged. Another question for the philosophers and theologians. There was nothing she could do about it. So why think about it? There were more important things to occupy her mind.

Such as Solomon.

She glanced up to the dais, where her

son stood near his father during the proceedings of the royal court. He was the only one of the princes in sight. Seldom did the others appear in court to take part in the affairs of the kingdom. Not even Adonijah, next in line to be king.

Where was Adonijah? Out with the troops, probably, practicing war. Or maybe parading through the streets of Jerusalem like Absalom used to do, proudly riding his chariot, with fifty young men leading the way, accepting the cheers of the people. He should be here now, learning the art of statecraft, preparing to govern his nation.

But he wasn't. And Solomon was.

The rumors still circulated that Solomon, not Adonijah, should be the next king of Israel. She resolved to speak to David about this at her next opportunity.

The opportunity arose that very evening. David, according to his custom, came to her room after the business of the evening had been completed. Tired and often discouraged by the burdens of the nation, he found rest and refreshment in Bathsheba's company.

"Those poor girls." His mind still struggled with the fate of the ten concubines he had sentenced to eternal spinsterhood. "But there wasn't anything else I could do.

Except execute them. And I couldn't do that."

"I know, David," she murmured.

"Solomon was there. I couldn't let him see me doing anything else. After all, I am the king." He sighed. "It's such a burden."

"And Solomon?" Bathsheba took his hand in hers. "What do you have in mind for his future?"

He looked at her, smiling sadly. "I don't know. What is Yahweh's will for him? I must ask Nathan."

"I'll talk to Nathan, if you like. I'll probably see him in the morning, in the courtyard."

Since their return to the palace a few days ago, Bathsheba and Nathan had resumed their early morning strolls together. They had spoken of many things — the palace intrigues, the daily court happenings, the reluctance of the northern tribes to accept David's resumption of the throne. But they had never discussed Solomon's future. And so in the morning she began her discussion with the aging prophet by asking a question.

"Honored sir," began Bathsheba, using the form of address proper for the respected seer. "The king wonders about his son Solomon. And so do I. What does his future hold? Have you any word from Yahweh?"

The old man nodded, gray beard bobbing on his rotund stomach. "There is, my dear. And the word is clear. Solomon will be the next king of Israel."

Bathsheba blinked. But she was not surprised. "Are you sure?" she asked, not wanting to accept it.

Again he nodded. "Yahweh has been preparing the boy for many years now. He has given Solomon wisdom beyond the measure of most men. He will be a great king — as great as his father."

"But what about Adonijah? And the other princes?"

Nathan shrugged. "Who can fathom the mind of Yahweh. I just accept his word; I don't try to understand it."

"But . . . to gain the throne — does that mean. . . ?"

The prophet's eyes flashed something of the fire he used to show in youth.

"It means Yahweh has not yet completed his chastisement of the king for his great sin. There is more to come."

Bathsheba shook her head. Tears rolled unbidden from her eyes. This was not what she wanted to hear. In her old age, she just wanted peace. Peace for herself — and her husband. Hadn't they suffered enough?

That night she reported to David the word from the prophet. He rubbed his graying beard with his thumb and forefinger, brow lowered in a frown.

"I'm surprised," he said. "Not that Solomon will be the next king. I think I've always known that. What surprises me is that God is still punishing me for my sin. When will it end? But I promise you I will do all I can to help him ascend to the throne. Peacefully. Without bloodshed."

"And Adonijah?"

David shrugged. "We'll see. Yahweh's will be done."

16

Resentment and rebellion festered among the northern tribes of Israel in the years following David's return to Jerusalem. They resented David's preferential treatment of the tribe of Judah. The king gave all the choice appointments to Judahites. They especially resented Amasa, the commander-in-chief who replaced Joab.

Through the years, Joab had remained loyal to the king. He and his brother Abishai had been made co-commanders of David's personal bodyguard, and Joab often grumbled about his demotion and the way Amasa handled the army. The new commander-in-chief was a great warrior, but as a general he was inadequate.

"If only Joab were in charge," so the widespread complaint went, "things would get done properly. The standing army is like a man without a head."

The army seemed to be divided into two factions: those who had followed Absalom in the rebellion, and those who remained loyal to David. Some of the loyalists finally had their fill of Amasa's leadership. They revolted.

A report came to David about the division and insurrection in the army. Seated on his throne in the Assembly Hall, he listened to the messenger, his face sad.

Finally he sighed. "I thought we had peace at last in Israel. Evidently not. Who's leading this rebellion?"

"A man of Benjamin, my king. Sheba ben Bichri."

"I never heard of him. Is he one of the old veterans who followed King Saul many years ago?"

"I don't know, my king."

"I know him, David." Joab stepped forward boldly and stood at the foot of the dais, facing his king. He had scarcely aged, Bathsheba noted as she stood in the back of the crowd of courtiers. Streaks of gray flecked his hair and beard, but he still stood erect and proud and walked without any noticeable limp, as many men his age did. His eyes still held the fire which reflected his inner nature. He only, of all the courtiers, addressed the king by his given name.

"How do you know him, Joab?" asked the king.

"He approached me not long ago. His own Benjaminites wouldn't even follow him, and he wanted me to lead the movement. I told him to tuck his tail between his legs and run off to the hills."

Bathsheba frowned. *You should have killed him. It's unlike you not to.*

Evidently David had the same thought. "Why didn't you kill him on the spot?" he asked.

"I wish now I had," growled Joab. "He was such a slimy old snake, I thought he would just slither back into the rocks."

Bathsheba smiled, and she noted grins on the faces of many of the other courtiers. They had not missed the quaint expressions of Joab's speech. First Sheba was a dog, then a snake.

"Let me take your bodyguard and go after this donkey," Joab said loudly. "I'll make him bray before I cut off his head!"

This time a few chuckles broke out among the assembly. Joab turned and glowered at those who didn't take his words seriously.

David shook his head. "No, not you, Joab. You'll only cause more upheaval, and all I want is peace. Amasa. Take a few warriors, and go put down this small insurrection. Use persuasion, not force. Where is this Sheba now?"

The messenger replied, "In Gibeon, my king."

Gibeon. A small town only a few miles northwest of Jerusalem. It shouldn't take long.

"Three days," said David softly. "That's all it should take you, Amasa. And . . . do it quietly. No trouble. Do you understand?"

"Yes, my king." Amasa turned and left the Assembly Hall.

He should have sent Joab and the bodyguard, thought Bathsheba. A quick, quiet assassination was Joab's style. Amasa would make a large production out of it.

Three days passed, and no word from Amasa. Then a week. David fumed.

"What is taking him so long?" he told Bathsheba one night in their bedroom. "He should have been back long ago."

"You should have allowed Joab to go. He could have done the job quickly. Besides, Joab needs something to do, some way you can show your confidence in him."

David grinned. "You sound like Solomon. That's what he told me last week."

"It's still not too late."

David shook his head. "I don't think it's wise to put Amasa and Joab together at the head of a small punitive assignment. Not even Abishai could keep peace between them."

"Are you sure it's still a small revolt? Maybe by this time it has grown to a full rebellion."

David rubbed his chin. "I don't know. But you may be right. I'll ask Nathan."

He had been successful in the past when he consulted the prophet for a word from Yahweh. He would do it again.

The next day, after consulting Nathan, David assigned Abishai the task of taking his bodyguard of veterans to Gibeon.

"Keep me informed," he charged his cousin. "Amasa has left me in the dark. I don't know what's going on."

"I will, my king."

"And please, keep Joab out of trouble. You know how he feels about Amasa. We have peace in Israel now. I'd like to keep it that way."

Two days later, a messenger arrived at the palace. From Abishai.

"Sheba has fled to the north," Abishai's messenger reported.

"And Amasa? What of him?"

"Dead, my king."

"By whose hand?"

Bathsheba shuddered when she heard

the question. She knew the answer.

"Joab's, my lord king."

Bathsheba heard the gasps of the courtiers in the Assembly Hall.

The messenger told the story. "Amasa had mobilized the army of Judah to follow the rebel Sheba. At Gibeon, he had encamped to organize and prepare for the campaign."

"Campaign?" David frowned. "This was just a small mission, not a major expedition."

The messenger gulped. He knew nothing about the larger picture. He knew only what he had seen and what Abishai had told him to say.

"When Joab met Amasa, he kissed him. At the same time he stabbed him in the stomach. His knife ripped open —"

Bathsheba shuddered and shut her ears. She didn't want to hear the gory details. But she could picture what had happened. Joab and Amasa had been companions of David from the beginning. They would greet each other with a kiss. And while Joab held the commander-in-chief's beard with one hand, his other hand would draw the dagger. . . . Again she shuddered.

"Then Abishai took his men and went north after Sheba. He left Amasa's body on the road, wallowing in blood. A young officer was stationed there to tell the army of Judah to take their choice — either follow Joab, or suffer the same fate as Amasa."

Seeing David frown, the messenger hurried on with his story. "Many of the Judahites hesitated there, staring at the body of Amasa, not sure what to do. So Abishai's officer pulled the body off to the side of the road and covered him with a robe. Then the Judahites just went on, following Abishai. But I came here to report to you, my king."

The outraged courtiers in the Assembly Hall all shouted at once that Joab should be recalled, even executed. But Joab wasn't there. He was miles away, in the north, and probably wouldn't come even if summoned.

"We'll wait," said David.

It was all he could do. Bathsheba, like everyone else, knew that Joab was the best man to deal with the rebellion. If successful, he might even earn forgiveness.

But as Solomon so cleverly put it later when talking with Bathsheba, "He may have tipped the boulder over the cliff this time."

One thing you could say about Joab.

Assassin that he was, he was loyal to David. And he kept his king informed. Almost every day a messenger arrived at the court with news from the front. And the reports indicated that Joab, not Abishai, was in charge.

Sheba and his rebels had moved far to the north, beyond the Sea of Chinnereth. They appeared to be only a small band of men, mostly from Sheba's own clan of Bichri. Evidently reports of the large numbers of Israelites involved in the insurrection had been false, or else they had melted away when they learned the army of Judah — and especially the king's elite bodyguard — had been called out to oppose them.

Word finally arrived that the prey had been brought to bay — in the walled city of Abel in Beth-maacah. Joab, experienced in this kind of warfare, built a siege ramp and prepared to level the walls of the city.

The reports from the front then brought a strange twist. "A woman appeared on the walls," reported the messenger, "asking for Joab. Specifically for Joab. And he went out and talked with her."

Bathsheba listened with interest to the young warrior's report in the Assembly Hall. The courtiers were silent, fascinated.

"The woman said to Joab, 'This is the city of Abel. For years our people have had a reputation for wisdom. And we have counseled many people. We've always been peaceful, and faithful to our king. So why do you seek to devour a city which has been a mother to Israel?' "

The phrase, "a mother to Israel," reminded Bathsheba of Deborah, the wise woman who judged Israel more than a century ago. She had been called mother to Israel.

David stood up, obviously impressed with the report of the wise woman's words. "I have heard of Abel, and its reputation for wisdom. Indeed, the city is a 'mother' in Israel. Many small towns around her turn to her for counsel and protection." He stroked his chin. "And how did Joab answer her?"

"My lord king," replied the messenger, "he replied, 'Far be it from me to devour any city! We only want one man who has taken refuge inside your walls. This man, Sheba ben Bichri, has rebelled against King David. If you give him up to us, we'll go and leave your city in peace!' "

David, still on his feet, took two steps forward on the dais. "And did she do as Joab asked?"

The soldier nodded. "Yes, sir. Just a few hours later, Sheba's head came sailing out over the wall and landed near where Joab stood."

David nodded. "And what did Joab do then?"

"He sounded the trumpet, my lord king. And we all retreated from the city. The troops are on their way home now, and I ran on ahead."

David's face broke into a broad smile. "Praise Yahweh! Let us prepare Jerusalem to celebrate the triumphant return of our troops! And let no man speak unfavorably against Joab, who is now — and always — my commander-in-chief!"

As the Assembly Hall rang with cheers and shouts of joy, Bathsheba studied her husband's face. He was obviously relieved that the rebellion was over. But even more, he was relieved that Joab had been vindicated. David had always loved his impulsive and unprincipled nephew, in spite of his many outrageous acts. The murders of Absalom and Amasa were forgiven.

When the army returned, the city became festive. As they entered the Valley Gate and marched down the broad avenue toward the palace, Bathsheba watched from the palace rooftop, along with the other wives. A mob of people lined the street, waving palm branches and shouting praises to Yahweh and David and Joab. Some even took off their cloaks and spread them on the street for Joab to march over.

Bathsheba sighed. Peace had come to Israel at last. She hoped this was the end of rebellions — and especially of Yahweh's punishment for David's sin.

17

Young Solomon bolted into maturity. Nobody called him a boy any more.

His silky black hair and beard gave his features a delicate mold, especially since he trimmed his beard short and pointed. His thin ascetic face made him look more a child of Bathsheba than David.

As Bathsheba looked at the young man, she could scarcely see any resemblance to his father. She wondered why no rumors floated around the palace about Solomon really being the son of Uriah the Hittite. This was impossible, since Solomon was the second son of David and Bathsheba, the first having died in childbirth. But when people spread rumors, they were seldom deterred by the facts.

And there were plenty of rumors. An old one said Daniel, Queen Abigail's son, was not David's offspring but son of Nabal, Abigail's first husband. It wouldn't surprise Bathsheba if similar rumors circulated about Solomon — perhaps originating from his enemies.

His enemies? Did Solomon have enemies? Possibly his half brother Adonijah, who surely heard the talk about Solomon succeeding his father to the throne in place of David's oldest son. Everybody seemed to be saying that now.

Bathsheba had finally accepted that Solomon should become the next king. It was Yahweh's will. The prophet Nathan said so. David said so. Even the respected counselor Hushai had said so — on his deathbed, and deathbed words were respected.

Everybody said so, it seemed, except Solomon. That young man said nothing. He wisely let others do the talking.

Several years before, at age seventeen, he had taken the warrior's training like all other young men in Israel. He endured it was what Bathsheba had heard. He was lithe and quick, and would fight with intelligence and skill, but his heart wasn't in it. He was a man of peace.

She recalled the proverb Solomon himself had originated many years ago. "He who must fight to settle his differences, does so because he isn't intelligent enough to settle them peacefully." A lot of proverbs were being ascribed to him these days, many of which he had never said. But she had heard him say this one more than once.

Solomon had taken his place among the counselors surrounding the throne. Solomon's sleek black hair stood out among all the gray beards. Yet he belonged there. Not just because he was the king's son and might well be the next king, but because his wisdom and wit had earned him respect and deference. The king obviously preferred his young son's counsel above all the others.

But what would Adonijah do? Would he meekly accept the widespread belief that Solomon was Yahweh's choice as next king? Not likely. That vain prince still paraded around Jerusalem in his chariot, accepting cheers, reminding everyone of Absalom. Some, if rumor could be believed, actually felt he would make a better king than Solomon, but they based that on his striking appearance and similarity to a young David more than his wisdom. He seldom appeared in the Assembly Hall while affairs of the kingdom were discussed.

Bathsheba wondered if her fears would materialize, that Solomon, to be king, would stride to the throne across the bloody bodies of his brothers. She shuddered. That would be the ultimate punishment from Yahweh on David for the sin which had already so clouded their otherwise happy marriage.

As David aged, his kingdom became more peaceful. There were no more uprisings, borders to secure, invasions by ambitious armies. When disputes arose between Israel and other nations, David settled them by diplomacy. Prosperity and contentment came to Israel, and this was reflected in the social life of the palace.

Bathsheba basked in the companionship of her sister wives, as well as the wives of David's companions and advisers. She had not known such fellowship since before her marriage. Shua was her best friend again. Most people called her "Queen Bathsheba," which gratified her but did not thrill her as much now as it would have when she was young. She valued the love and friendship they gave her more than the honors.

The courtyard had become once more her favorite place to spend the days. There the women gathered and gossiped while the men conducted the affairs of the kingdom in the Assembly Hall. Often the women had the nation's problems solved while the men were still arguing.

One day David's wife Haggith approached Bathsheba. Like all the other original wives of David, Haggith had thickened in the middle, turned gray, and showed wrinkles on her face. Her steps were slow and painful.

"Queen Bathsheba." That Haggith would use this term showed not only her acceptance of Bathsheba's position, but also a touch of fear. She was, after all, the mother of Adonijah.

Bathsheba smiled. "Yes, Haggith? Is all well with you?"

"Yes, my queen." Haggith hesitated, then continued, her voice agitated. "Well, no, my lady. It's . . . well, you know as well as I do that our sons are rivals for the throne. When our lord the king dies, one will replace him."

Bathsheba nodded. That Haggith would bring this up showed her obvious concern. They had studiously avoided the subject before.

"May I . . . well . . . make a suggestion. When one of our sons is king — whichever one it is — let there still be friendship between us. Let there be . . . peace."

Bathsheba nodded. She understood what Haggith was trying to say. When rival factions contended for the throne and one succeeded, the loser and his supporters should be executed to avoid future uprisings. It happened in most nations. It could happen here.

"I can assure you, Haggith, there will be peace." She smiled, trying to calm the worried lady who stood before her clasping and unclasping her hands. "Both our sons are too wise to settle their problems by washing them away with brother's blood. Or motherblood, for that matter."

"Yes. I agree." Haggith retained the worried look, and Bathsheba knew she was still not reassured. "Let there be peace between us. And if you will speak to Solomon, I will speak to Adonijah. Let there be peace."

As Haggith turned away, Bathsheba frowned. What had led her to approach Bathsheba today? Did she know something nobody else did?

She glanced around the courtyard. Did anybody know anything? Everyone seemed to be chatting and laughing as usual. She shrugged. Just the worries and confusion of old age. Everything was all right —

The tranquillity of the courtyard was shattered by the sudden appearance of Nathan. He strode into the courtyard — hobbled, rather, for his old legs could scarcely hold him. Nevertheless he seemed to stride, for the old fire and vigor were still in his eyes.

The courtyard became silent as the women turned to stare at him. Some gaped and others cringed.

"Get out!" roared the prophet, his voice as commanding as ever. "All of you, get out — now!"

Hastily the women bustled out, going into the palace through the nearest door. All but Bathsheba. She suspected that the prophet was there to talk to her. And because of their friendship, she seemed to be the only woman in the palace who did not fear this awesome seer.

Nathan's fiery eyes softened when he saw her. He hobbled over to where Bathsheba sat on a bench.

"My lady," he said, and Bathsheba caught the agitation in his voice. "It has begun."

"What has begun, my lord Nathan?"

Nathan's lips moved nervously over his toothless gums; his gray beard jutted forward.

"Adonijah. Haggith's son. He is now king of Israel."

"What?" Bathsheba stood up. "What do you mean?"

"This very day, he has proclaimed him-

189

self king, and the priest Abiathar has anointed him with the holy oil. Our lord David doesn't even know about it yet."

Bathsheba gasped, recalling what Haggith had said to her just a few moments before. Had she known?

Nathan's next words slapped her like a blow of his hand.

"Your life is in danger, my lady. And the life of your son Solomon."

Then Haggith's words were not merely a benign wish on her part. The threat to the loser in this power struggle was real.

"What . . . what should we do?" she asked.

"You must do exactly as I say." Nathan swayed on his feet as he bent his head slightly toward her. "Go to the king. At once. And say to him, 'Didn't you promise me that our son Solomon would be the next king? Why is Adonijah now claiming the throne of Israel?' Then, while you're still talking, I'll come in and tell him the same thing."

As Bathsheba climbed the stairs to the third floor bedroom, she trembled. Fear? Yes. But excitement also. She felt sure Yahweh intended Solomon to be king. Was this to be the fulfillment of his destiny? Was the drama to be played out on the stage of Israel's history this very day?

18

David was in the bedroom today. He had not tried to make his way to the Assembly Hall to conduct the business of the kingdom. He stayed in his room frequently these days, because his health in his declining years confined him mostly to the large bedroom. The affairs of state were often conducted right here, in the Queen's Room, which was often a busy place.

Fortunately at this moment David was resting. While a few people stood around the walls or in the hall, they kept quiet, waiting for the king to renew his strength to continue his business. Nobody stood beside the bed as Bathsheba entered.

"My lord husband," she said gently, sitting on the bed beside him.

He opened his eyes instantly. Evidently he had not been sleeping. She knew he didn't sleep much these days.

"Send the others out of the room," she whispered. "I have something important to tell you."

David's voice rose as he commanded all to leave. He might not have much strength in his body, Bathsheba thought, but he still had a powerful voice — and will. He had given this order without hesitation just because she asked him, reflecting his love and respect for her.

"What do you want?" he asked gently, when everyone had gone.

She took a deep breath. "My lord husband, do you remember your oath before Yahweh that Solomon would be the next king of Israel?"

He nodded and said nothing.

She continued. "Well, you may not know it yet, but Adonijah has just proclaimed himself king."

"What?"

David raised up in bed. She helped him become more comfortable against the pillows.

"It's true, my husband. The priest Abiathar has just anointed him. So now Adonijah is king of Israel, unless you do something. Quickly."

David stared out the window, thumb and forefinger massaging his chin. His beard now was entirely gray, and not even the oil he used hid the thinning of his hair.

"All Israel is watching you at this

moment, my husband. You must do something — now — because everyone is waiting for your word. Who is to be next king of Israel?"

David continued to stare away from her. His eyes under his gray bushy brows looked out through narrow slits. Still he said nothing.

"It's more than that, David." She hesitated but plunged on. "Solomon and I — well, our lives are in danger. You know what happens to the family of the rival faction who loses when the king sleeps with his fathers. We . . . we will be counted as offenders."

"My lord king!" Sheva, David's young scribe, had just entered the room. "The prophet — Nathan — he insists on seeing you."

David nodded, but before he could say anything, Nathan pushed his way into the room. He teetered slightly as he gave a perfunctory bow before his king.

"My lord the king. Have you proclaimed your son Adonijah king in your place? Is he the one you have chosen to succeed you to the throne of Israel?"

David turned to look at his prophet.

Before he could speak, Nathan continued. "Listen to what your son Adonijah has done. He went out to En Rogel this morning. There he offered a huge sacrifice: many oxen, fat goats, sheep. He invited important people to be there, including Joab. And Abiathar the priest has anointed him king with the holy oil. They are celebrating, and shouting, 'Long live King Adonijah!' "

David bowed his head and shut his eyes. Bathsheba, watching his face, saw the mouth tighten and the jaw set.

Finally he opened his eyes and spoke. "Bathsheba."

"Yes, my husband?"

"By Yahweh, the living God, I swear to you once again that our son Solomon shall sit on the throne of Israel. I will see to it — today."

"Thank you, my love. May the king live forever."

She had used the formula address to the king, and he grunted as he heard the words. He of all people would know his own mortality.

He called Sheva the scribe and issued orders to summon Solomon and the elders who were present in Jerusalem. Also Benaiah, captain of his elite bodyguard. And Zadok, the other priest.

"Go," he told them, voice ringing with

authority. "Go to Gihon Spring. Gather the people as you go. Anoint Solomon with the holy oil, and proclaim him king of Israel. My choice for king. Then sound the trumpet and return through the streets of Jerusalem shouting 'Long live Solomon, the new king of Israel!' "

Benaiah, captain of the bodyguard, spoke for all of them. "Praise Yahweh!" he shouted. "As God has been with the present king, so may he be with the new one! And may Solomon's reign be even greater than yours!"

His shout ignited a chorus of agreement, and the excited company left the room to go about their mission.

David leaned back on his pillows, face pale and strained. He reached out his hand, and Bathsheba instantly grasped it.

"Go to the roof of the palace," he whispered. "Watch what happens. Then come and tell me."

"I will, my husband."

As she left him to go to the rooftop, she sighed. It had happened. Her son would be co-regent with his father now. But . . . could he do it without bloodshed?

From the rooftop, Bathsheba could look out across Jerusalem. At first she saw in the southeast a plume of smoke, which she knew to be coming from En Rogel in the Kidron Valley. That would be the remains of the sacrifice offered just this morning by the priest Abiathar, following the anointing of Adonijah. She shuddered. Two anointings in one day. That could only mean bloodshed.

She turned to the northeast, to the Water Gate, where so many great events had taken place. She couldn't see beyond the city wall, because there the road dipped sharply into the valley before climbing the Mount of Olives. In this valley was the Gihon Spring, where David had directed his people to go for Solomon's anointing.

She waited. The sun overhead blazed while a mist of dust rose from the city. The dry season had established itself. Nevertheless she could see clearly enough to know when the new sacrifice would be offered at Gihon.

It seemed a long wait. Finally she saw a thin plume of white smoke. Then she heard the sound she had anticipated — a long plaintive trumpet blast. The shophar sounded positive, almost cheerful. Two notes, ending with the higher pitched one, sounding festive. Something good was being announced. Then other trumpets joined, and Bathsheba could hear the shouting. She kept her eyes on the Water Gate, looking for the first appearance of the triumphant return.

She didn't have long to wait. The parade emerged from the gate. First came several priests, blowing trumpets. Solomon came next, riding a mule — the white mule reserved for the king alone. The mule was led by Benaiah, captain of the king's bodyguard.

Behind Solomon came a large mass of people, with some of the most important men in the kingdom following proudly behind their new king. As the procession marched through the winding city streets, taking the long way to the palace, crowds of people joined them. And they cheered.

Bathsheba was able to distinguish their shouts, mainly because she knew what to listen for. *Long live King Solomon!* Did they make more noise than Adonijah's company had? What would the people think, seeing two coronations in one day?

Even more important, what would Adonijah think? And Joab? Who knew what Joab would do. He might even now be plotting assassination.

She had seen enough. It was time to report to David. She made her way downstairs, thankful her report would at least be good news. The crowd which followed Solomon was large — and loud.

David received her report passively, indeed stolidly, almost as if he knew it was not over yet. What would Adonijah do? What would happen next in the drama of creating a new king of Israel?

The answer came a few hours later. Solomon had come directly to the Queen's Room with Zadok the priest, Nathan the prophet, and many of David's companions and advisers. Benaiah and his bodyguard had stationed themselves at strategic entrances to the palace. David's spies canvassed the city for news of Adonijah. Now they could do nothing but wait. But they were ready.

Ahimaaz, the son of Zadok the priest, brought the news. He burst into the room, shouting. "My lord king! Your son Adonijah has fled to the tabernacle. I saw him there myself. He has taken hold of the horns of the altar and is pleading for mercy."

Shouts of joy echoed across the room as the people pictured what had happened. Bathsheba, from her position against the wall near David's bedside, saw that picture in her imagination.

Although she had never seen the horns of the altar, she knew they were knobs on the sacred altar inside the large tent of the tabernacle. Some denounced these ornaments as carryovers from pagan worship, but they had been there since the tabernacle was erected early in David's reign.

Adonijah had grasped the horns. That meant he sought sanctuary, refuge from the wrath of Solomon. Bathsheba pictured him there, cringing, begging for mercy.

Ahimaaz confirmed that picture. "I myself went into the tabernacle and spoke to him. He asked me to tell you that he is sorry for all the trouble he has caused. His very words, my king, were, 'Tell King Solomon I will not leave this altar until he swears an oath that he will not kill me!' "

Two things struck Bathsheba about Ahimaaz's report. One was that he addressed himself to David, not Solomon. Good. As long as David lived, he was still king, with Solomon only co-king.

The other was what Adonijah had called Solomon. *King Solomon.* The men in the room grasped the significance of this title on Adonijah's lips, for they shouted and waved their arms for joy. Even David smiled as he lay back, relaxed, on his pillows.

Everyone rejoiced, that is, except Solomon. That young man stood by the bed, his face a mask of seriousness. He frowned as he rubbed his chin with his thumb and forefinger in his father's characteristic gesture.

The room quieted as the men realized their new co-king did not rejoice as they did. Bathsheba shuddered as she watched her son. Would he begin his reign with the blood of his brother, as she had feared?

When Solomon spoke, his voice seemed ice-cold. Bathsheba realized this was his first order as co-king of Israel.

"If he acts with worthy submission," he said slowly, "I will not harm one hair of his head. But . . . if he turns his hand to sedition one more time, he shall die."

Bathsheba breathed a sigh of relief. His first act, then, was mercy. But the mercy was tempered with a stern warning.

She nodded, admiring his wisdom. The new king had just given notice to all that he would be a kind king, like his father. But not a gullible king. He seemed to be saying to all: *Be careful. I am merciful, but I will not tolerate anyone taking advantage of this mercy.*

19

Now that Solomon sat on the throne of Israel, David relaxed and submitted to the weaknesses of old age. He remained in bed most of the time. Occasionally on warm days he would ask to be carried down to the courtyard where he could lie in the sun.

Solomon conducted the business of the kingdom now, and he did it well, if the stories could be believed. His reputation for wisdom spread over the earth.

David listened when reports were given him about Solomon's actions, but he seemed to have no interest in the kingdom any more. Only one matter absorbed him now: building the Temple for Yahweh.

Bathsheba recalled the time several years before when David proclaimed his burning desire to build the Temple.

"It isn't right," he was often heard to say, "that I should dwell in a magnificent palace, while my God lives in a tent."

It became a focal point of his kingship. He had wanted to begin construction immediately, but Yahweh, through his prophet Nathan, had said no. David, always obedient, had submitted to Yahweh's will.

That was before Absalom rebelled, even before David had married Bathsheba. It was, in fact, in the days before David's troubles began.

As Bathsheba looked back across the years, she felt she understood why David was so concerned about the construction of the Temple now.

His troubles began, it seemed, with his marriage to Bathsheba. From the night he had commanded her to come to him on the palace rooftop, then ordered Uriah's death, Yahweh had begun his punishment. And from David's point of view, that punishment had never ended.

David had become a different person. He felt strongly the burden of guilt. Strange, that it had not affected Bathsheba that way. She had experienced Yahweh's forgiveness. Any guilt she had was wiped away when Nathan the prophet had helped her see that God offered her only love and not condemnation. But what of David?

Bathsheba saw it clearly now. David had not known the peace which had come to her. He had felt the weight of his sin through the years. All his afflictions he attributed to Yahweh's wrath. When his son Absalom rebelled and was killed in the rebellion, he suffered greatly. He thought Yahweh would then make an end to the punishments. But to his tortured mind, God had continued them.

When famine came to the nation of Israel — indeed, to all the world — David believed Yahweh was still inflicting his wrath on him. The Chronicler had written that the famine was punishment for the sin of taking a census. Nobody fully believed that. Especially David. He clung to the belief that Yahweh still punished him for his one great sin.

Yes, mused Bathsheba. It disturbed David greatly that he could not build the Temple. It added an even heavier load to his guilt. Even though he had decided to delay construction before he committed his great sin, his twisted mind somehow believed this too was part of Yahweh's punishment.

Now, in his old age, he was more convinced than ever. The only way Israel would be cleansed of his great sin, he told Bathsheba one day, was through building the Temple.

"I have done what I could," he said.

"Solomon our son is young and tender. He shall build the house for Yahweh. And he will bring Yahweh's peace to Israel."

David's days now were absorbed in preparing for the building of the Temple. It was the only project in which he took even the slightest interest.

Large supplies of cedar were imported from Lebanon. His old friend King Hiram had sent him everything he needed to begin the long-awaited project. This included not only materials but architects and craftsmen. Now all was ready — except for one thing. David's death.

When Solomon came to visit him, the only thing David spoke of was building the Temple. "Let it be your first project, my son," he told the young king. "Yahweh has given you wisdom. You can see how important this is. If you do this, Yahweh will bless Israel. Not only in your lifetime, but throughout the reign of all your descendants, forever."

And Solomon promised — even swore an oath before Yahweh — that it would be done.

20

When the *yoreh* arrived, the first rain of the cold season, David would not even come down to the courtyard any more. He never left his bed.

"I'm cold," he told Bathsheba, and his trembling limbs and chattering teeth confirmed his statement.

Several doctors attended him constantly. He had physicians not only from Israel, but from Egypt and Syria and even Babylonia. They could do nothing for him.

"He is dying," they told Bathsheba. "Only Yahweh can save him now." She smiled at their references to Yahweh, knowing the foreign doctors had their own deities.

A brazier was lit near the bed with a charcoal fire to provide some warmth. But the fumes made him cough, and he ordered it taken away. Blankets were piled on top of him, until their weight was so heavy he had trouble breathing. They tried wrapping his limbs with damp cloths soaked in boiling water, but that burned his delicate skin. They put heated stones in his bed, but blisters rose on the soles of his sensitive feet.

Finally Benaiah came up with an ingenious suggestion. The aging captain of the bodyguard had been with David from the beginning. He had remained loyal to the king while many others — including Joab — had deserted him. Benaiah came almost daily to the bedroom to express concern for his king's health.

When he saw David lying on the pillows, teeth chattering, Benaiah's face clouded with sorrow. "My king," he whispered. "What can I do?"

David shook his head. "Nothing, my friend. You cannot make me warm."

Benaiah tried to revive the king's interest in the Temple-building project, but even that had ceased to be foremost in the king's mind. After a while Benaiah rose and turned to leave.

"Bathsheba," he whispered. "Walk with me."

Out in the hall, he asked her, "Can nothing be done for the king? He's so cold!"

Bathsheba told him about all the attempts the physicians had made to warm him. Benaiah listened, face somber.

"Try one more thing," he said. "Find a young virgin to be his concubine. She might warm him up."

Bathsheba shook her head. "It won't do any good. He hasn't taken any new concubines since before Absalom's rebellion. Those ten young women spoiled by Absalom were the last. And . . . he has no desire. I should know."

Benaiah nodded. "Nevertheless, a young concubine would not do any harm. She might warm his body, if nothing else."

After the captain of the bodyguard had gone, Bathsheba went in to David. She told him Benaiah's suggestion. To her surprise, he approved.

"It can do no harm," he muttered. "I'll try anything."

The search began. Benaiah himself took charge of the project. He called together the old companions of David, those left of the Mighty Thirty.

"Go into all the country," he told them, "and find the most beautiful girl in the land. This will be the last act of devotion we can do for our beloved king."

It must have been a strange sight, mused Bathsheba, to see all these venerable soldiers plodding through the country, or riding their donkeys, gray beards hanging to their rounded stomachs, asking to see the most beautiful girls in the land. Nevertheless, the reports she heard from the ancient warriors were encouraging. Everywhere fathers volunteered their daughters to be candidates for the king's last concubine.

Each of the old men sent out on the mission brought home one young virgin of his choice. Benaiah and Bathsheba reviewed them. They were all beautiful, personable, vivacious.

Finally they chose one. She was an Issacharite, from the village of Shunem at the edge of the Plain of Jezreel. A dark-haired slim maiden, she had long, fluttery eyelashes which blinked charmingly. Her broad mouth smiled warmly and often. They interviewed her and learned she was eager to serve her king.

She told them her name. Abishag. It sounded so much like "Abigail" they thought David might be confused. So they decided to call her simply "The Shunemite."

They brought her to David that very night. Bathsheba stayed only long enough to see her crawl under the covers beside him. He enfolded her in his arms. Then

Bathsheba and all the others discreetly left them alone.

Bathsheba was surprised that she felt little jealousy. She had never felt the envy she should have for the wives David had married or the concubines he had taken. That was the custom of the land, and in fact was followed by all kings everywhere. The law of Moses, while proclaiming monogamy as the ideal, nevertheless sanctioned polygamy and the taking of concubines for the purpose of bearing sons and continuing the family name. The law of Moses was especially lenient toward kings, merely cautioning them not to place too much emphasis on the number of wives and concubines in the royal household.

What mattered most to Bathsheba was love. David had often expressed his love for her. He had never loved anyone else, with the exception of Abigail. Even now, when desire had failed in her husband's old age, she was assured of his continuing love. And love was different from lust.

Bathsheba was certain David would not revive his sexual desires with the nubile virgin in his bed. But if her young vibrant body could produce some warmth in his, it would be the best medicine possible.

Early the next morning, Bathsheba went

to the bedroom. David slept soundly.

The young Shunemite slipped out of bed and dressed hurriedly. Her face was troubled.

"How did he do?" asked Bathsheba.

She sighed. "He seemed to be comfortable, and he slept fairly well. But. . . ."

"But what?"

The young face clouded. "I'm not sure . . . that is, I think . . . well, he doesn't want me in his bed any more."

"Why do you say that?"

"It was something he said during the night."

"What did he say?" demanded Bathsheba.

"He said, 'We mustn't do this, my love. It's against the law of Moses.' "

Bathsheba smiled, relaxing. She knew exactly what he meant.

"That was not meant for you, child. You know how old people are — or maybe you don't. His mind wanders. He was referring to something in the past. Some babbling dream which has nothing to do with you."

Her calm assurance set the Shunemite's mind at ease, and she spoke no more of it. In fact, as soon as David awakened, she shed her clothes and crawled back into bed beside him. He accepted her in his arms gratefully.

Bathsheba felt an overwhelming relief. The girl was doing some good after all. Not the way the physicians had expected, for that was beyond his strength in his advanced age. But his body had warmed somewhat, and he was a little more comfortable.

Bathsheba frowned as she thought about what her husband had said to the Shunemite during the night. She recalled vividly that first month of their great sin, when Uriah still lived, and Bathsheba visited David every night on the palace roof. He had spoken to her those same words.

Against the law of Moses, he had said. The law of Moses regarding adultery, not taking concubines.

So David still bore the burden of guilt. Even when he was only half-conscious.

21

It became apparent to all that David would not live through the rainy season, despite the Shunemite's warming treatments. Even David knew it.

"Bring Solomon to me," he told Bathsheba one day. "I want to give him my blessing."

When Solomon arrived, David sent everyone out of the room except the Shunemite. He would not endure the cold even to have a few moments of privacy with his son.

He spent more than an hour with Solomon. When the young king finally emerged from the room, his face was grim. He refused to speak about what his father had told him.

Bathsheba guessed the blessing had something to do with building the Temple. If he made that his highest priority, Yahweh would continue the Promise through him and his descendants. The Promise was that Israel would be a great nation. The land would be theirs forever. And through his descendants, all people on earth would be blessed.

The days passed with agonizing slowness. Most of the time, David slept. The Shunemite seemed to be always in his bed. Even when visitors lined the walls of the room, she remained there, clinging to him.

Bathsheba stayed with him also. She tended his needs and often asked that the room be cleared. The needs of a dying man were much too personal and embarrassing to be on public display. When that happened, they gathered in the hallway, waiting, conversing in whispers, dispersing gloom to all in the household.

Bathsheba was grateful for Benaiah's help. The faithful captain of the bodyguard seemed constantly present, enforcing her rules, driving the company of men into the hallway when she needed privacy. At night, he made sure everyone went home except Bathsheba, the Shunemite, and a physician. Benaiah himself camped in the hallway, always on guard.

Bathsheba shared the bed with David at night. With the Shunemite on one side and Bathsheba on the other, David's emaciated body relaxed and he slept. At least his shivering and chattering had ceased. But the rale in his throat continued.

One night Bathsheba awakened suddenly and sat up in bed. What had wakened her? She looked around the room. All was quiet. The lamps flickered on their shelves around the room. The physician dozed in the corner. Everything seemed normal.

Then she looked down at David. He lay on his pillow with the Shunemite entwined around his body. But he was awake and staring up at her.

"Bathsheba, my love," he whispered.

She knew he was fully conscious, then, and had somehow pulled his mind together. She had heard that just before death, a moment of consciousness comes upon a person. Was this that moment?

The Shunemite slept soundly with the healthy abandon of youth. A feeling of peace came upon Bathsheba as she realized this was her last intimate moment with her beloved.

"I am here, my husband."

She lay back on the pillows, her face close to his. She could smell the fetid breath from his mouth, the breath of death. But there was no rattle in his throat. And the eyes that watched her were clear.

"David," she whispered. "I have loved

you always, ever since we first came together on the palace rooftop."

She wondered if her words would probe his memory and remind him of his guilt before Yahweh. He smiled and whispered something so softly she couldn't hear. She bent her head closer so her ear almost touched his lips. She heard his faint breathing and knew he was speaking words, but so faintly she could not make them out.

Then one phrase became clear: ". . . as far as the east is from the west. . . ."

A surge of joy swept through her. She knew exactly what he was saying.

One of his psalms was on his lips, a song he had composed many years ago, shortly after his great sin. The psalm reflected his hope that Yahweh would lift the burden of guilt which weighed so heavily on him. A forlorn hope. The burden had never left him.

Until now. She could tell by looking at his face the relief he felt.

She recalled the psalm David now was singing, even though he could do little more than move his lips. It sang in soft tones the love of Yahweh, who does not deal with us as we deserve. *As far as the east is from the west, so far does he remove our transgressions from us.*

And now — at last — David experienced that forgiveness!

She had felt it long ago. Nathan's loving counsel had allowed her to live without guilt. But not David. His very nature would not allow him to accept God's mercy. Perhaps this too was a part of the wise plan of Yahweh, for this burden of guilt had driven David to greater righteousness and more conscientious service to his God.

And Yahweh, in his wisdom, had removed the guilt. Now. At the moment of his servant's death.

She smiled. Her husband lay dying beside her, and she could smile. Her spirits soared, and she gazed fondly into his eyes. He returned the look, smiling. They understood each other.

She would not mourn his death. Yes, she would tear her clothes, strew dust on her head, and wail as loudly as anybody. She would shed tears and openly express her grief. But in her deepest self she would not mourn but would instead rejoice.

Again David tried to speak. She bent closer.

". . . Valley . . . of the shadow. . . ."

She recognized this psalm also. The

Shepherd Psalm. The one she knew would bring comfort and peace to many people in the future, just as it did for her now.

He was unable to finish his song. She smiled through tears. Not in this life, anyway.

ABOUT THE AUTHOR

JAMES R. SHOTT, a retired Presbyterian minister, says he is fascinated by the stories and characters in the Old Testament.

"These are real people," he notes. "They loved and were loved. They had likes and dislikes. They became involved in complicated and embarrassing and agonizing situations. They felt deeply about things. And always, like us, they struggled with their faith and came to appreciate or reject the God who ruled their lives. These are the people I write about."

Shott's Herald Press series, The People of the Promise — *Leah, Hagar, Joseph, Esau, Deborah, Othniel, Abigail, Bathsheba* — brings these Old Testament people alive.

Shott attends First Presbyterian Church in Palm Bay, Florida, where he lives with his wife, Esther. They enjoy watching their grandchildren grow up.

The employees of Thorndike Press hope you have enjoyed this Large Print book. All our Thorndike and Wheeler Large Print titles are designed for easy reading, and all our books are made to last. Other Thorndike Press Large Print books are available at your library, through selected bookstores, or directly from us.

For information about titles, please call:

(800) 223-1244

or visit our Web site at:

www.gale.com/thorndike
www.gale.com/wheeler

To share your comments, please write:

Publisher
Thorndike Press
295 Kennedy Memorial Drive
Waterville, ME   04901